Surrender Value

Why has John Everard, a gentle-mannered teacher of old-fashioned outlook surrendered an insurance policy and vanished? Is it really because, as he has told his wife, he fears a deterioration in his health and wants to go out 'living it up' in his own way? Have the tensions in a permissive sixth form college got him down? Did other women in his life really matter to him?

Or has he absconded with one of his pupils, prim little Susan Shires, who has also disappeared? Why has Sue dumped her bag and booked a double room at a sleazy London hotel?

Kenworthy, now retired from the Yard, is called in by Mrs Everard and finds himself exploring a world of some strange values. Meanwhile, reports on missing persons all over the country are being collated. Are Everard and Sue indulging in love-hate tantrums up and down the Norfolk coast? Or are they in the West Country, being turned away by suspicious landladies?

The mystery is not simplified when a girl's body in Sue's clothes is found in two different places. Kenworthy, working for a change as unofficial assistant to his former side-kick Shiner Wright, breaks this one by his familiar mixture of leaping imagination, bizarre deception — and by his instinct for the motives behind human eccentricities.

D1326771

JOHN BUXTON HILTON

Surrender Value

A Superintendent Kenworthy Novel

COLLINS, ST JAMES'S PLACE, LONDON

William Collins Sons & Co. Ltd
London · Glasgow · Sydney · Auckland
Toronto · Johannesburg

68510944

First published 1981
© John Buxton Hilton, 1981

ISBN 0 00 231795 8

Photoset in Compugraphic Baskerville
Printed in Great Britain by
T. J. Press (Padstow) Ltd

CHAPTER 1

There were people who went about noticing such things; it was a pity they kept them to themselves — until afterwards.

Jenny Arnold, twenty-three, hotel receptionist, technical college trained: at the moment when Joseph Kite (as he signed himself) was filling in his registration slip she had had four other craft in midstream. She'd had two phones off the hook; a guest asking directions to Upper Sheringham; an American woman talking about an eighteenth-century forbear who had been a blacksmith at North Walsham, and whose contemporary relatives she seemed to expect everyone in Norfolk to know.

So Jenny hadn't paid much attention to the couple, really, just told them where to find their room, the Ambassadeurs not running to a porter out of season. When she'd seen them approaching, she'd thought they'd be two singles, and she'd have to say no because of the Congress. Father and daughter, she'd have said, and the girl not long out of school, if out of school at all. But he said he'd made a reservation, though he'd lost the confirmation; and she'd had a job finding the booking, because of the temporary girl they'd had on last week. He'd signed as a married couple, and that was their business.

They had gone straight up to their room — Number 29, country view (the hotel yard) and no one had seen them again until half an hour before dinner. Then he'd come down alone into the bar and amused himself for twenty minutes at the fruit-machine before she'd appeared. Mike Doherty, barman and Ulsterman, described him as serious-looking and reluctant to converse. It was fairly obvious that he hadn't had much experience with fruit-machines. This one was the kind that featured a lit-up Bingo panel, and Doherty had had to come round the counter to show him how to catch the winning numbers with the hold buttons.

Mrs Marge Hogben — Mrs, but Hogben was her maiden name — had taken them their morning tea and the *Telegraph*, and he was asleep in the armchair in his dressing-gown. She was still sleeping too, right across the double bed, corner to corner, with the sheets pulled up over her head.

Old Mrs Frost, a motherly soul, had served them their breakfast. She'd also have said they were father and daughter, till she saw the ring on the girl's wedding finger. Very loose, it was. She remembered thinking, she'd have to watch she didn't pull it off with her gloves. The girl had looked rather poorly at the breakfast table. Sort of pale. Sort of as if she'd had a bad night. He looked such a quiet, decent, considerate sort of chap; but you couldn't always tell.

Then he'd settled his bill, notes from his wallet, fives and tens, and they went for a walk round the town and on the pier before he came back for his car: its number was such a scrawl on the hotel registration slip that you couldn't read it. Maybe you were not intended to.

On the pier, all its attractions bleakly closed down for the winter, they'd been seen by Walter Fothergill, carpenter, who was taking measurements for repairs to the children's helter-skelter. And he'd seen them go into Gypsy Rosanna's. Not that Rosie-Anne would have been in her booth in the normal run of events, only she was waiting for an electrician who was coming to rewire the place before next Easter opening.

No. Gypsy Rosanna — her West Riding accent contrasted flatly with the East Anglian vowels all round her — wasn't usually open for consultation at this time of the year, but the kid seemed to set such store by having her palm read. And who was going to turn down an unexpected quid?

The detective-sergeant who had traced the trail as far as the end of the pier reflected that palmists seemed to think that their prognostications were governed by the same code as applied to the confessional.

'I should think not indeed. I told them I had a full house. I mean, you can hardly ask to see people's marriage lines these days, can you? I just didn't like the look of them, that's all. He was nervous. Not the sort of man who could tell a lie without giving himself away. And she was a saucy young trollop. When I said no, she looked at me that hard-faced. She knew what I was thinking, right enough. It isn't always fair to blame the men, you know. But he did look of an age to know better. I mean, fifty, fifty-five. And I'd have put him down as a bank clerk or something. I'd have got on to you people straight away, but I mean, what had I to go on? If only I could have talked it over with my husband, but he was away on a business trip. And he would have created, if he'd thought I'd got on to you for nothing. It was only when I saw it in the paper this morning, I thought to myself, that could be them.'

She was a middle-aged woman who did bed-and-breakfasts on the edge of a West Country town.

'Now look, guv, this is a well-kept house. If we don't like the look of people, we don't take them in. I turn away thirty a day.'

It was a hotel in a side street to the north-west of Euston Station. Its office was a desk behind a glass door in a sort of hole under the stairs. The day manager had an anchor tattooed on each forearm.

'I mean, you can never be certain of a girl's age these days, but I'd put this one down as not a day more than sixteen. Nicely dressed: wearing a skirt. Rather angelic looking, in fact, with long hair and a green and white knitted tammy hat. She came in the middle of the morning and said she'd pay in advance and would like to leave her bag. When she said she wanted a double room, you could have buggered me through my oilskins. Then she looked at me a bit on the crafty side and said she'd have a girl-friend with her, and they wouldn't be in much before midnight. So I thought, well, that holds water, and she paid cash down. And never showed up. So the bag's still here, and what with the bloody IRA, and God knows what might be in unaccompanied luggage—'

The detective-constable—the call was at the moment rated no higher—took charge of the suitcase, which was cheap but new: plastic that might retain its imitation leather finish for a journey or two. It was locked, but he carried a useful keyring. He rummaged loosely through the girl's things: one spare blouse, one spare skirt, worn bedroom slippers, a packet of sanitary towels, already broached. Inside the neckband of most of the clothing was a nametape: *Susan C. Shires*: Gothic characters, machine-printed—obligatory, no doubt, by the rules of some school.

There were one or two books lying on top of the clothes: Bede's *Life and Miracles of St Cuthbert*, a heavily annotated edition of Chaucer's *Prologue*, a tattered text of *Samson Agonistes*.

'You wouldn't get much for this second-hand in Old Compton Street.'

The DC took the case with him.

CHAPTER 2

Kenworthy let himself be ushered into the house with a show of silent respect for its cold immaculacy: a smell of furniture polish so strong it was almost sickening. Not a newspaper in sight, not an ashtray that looked as if anything had ever been dropped in it, not a cushion that looked as if it had ever been sat on. Kenworthy sat on one of them now — when he was invited to. She'd fluff it out again the moment he was gone: if she didn't actually send it away to be fumigated.

She looked that sort of woman: tall, austere, unquestioningly certain of everything she said. She would be in her early fifties, hair two-to-one grey and black, bobbed, trimmed into geometrical curves at the sides of her ears; bifocal lenses in rims so narrow that it seemed doubtful whether they had rims at all.

There was clinical orderliness on mantelpiece, side-tables and in the glass-fronted bookcase-bureau. Yet there was not a single piece of furniture that was worth much in its own right. One or two pieces were not more than a decade or so old, but they had all come from standard catalogues. There had probably been a spasm of minor replacements after the children had left home — and in the wake of a pay rise — but it was a household founded on an inadequate nucleus of immediate post-second-war utility. It had never got itself abreast of the times. There had never been a margin to afford independent taste: it was a home kept impeccable on a schoolmaster's income. The only sign of active use was in the books on the home-made shelving between the chimney-breast and the outside wall: mostly under-graduate texts of pre-war vintage: modern languages, with a preponderance of early nineteenth-century texts. There were a few German publications of the 'fifties, but hardly anything contemporary, except for best-selling Grass and Böll. It was the room of a man who badly needed a den, but who was constrained by their three-bedroomed semi into not overflowing from his corner of what his wife called (Kenworthy did not wince) her lounge.

'I will do my best not to harrass you, Mrs Everard.'

'Of course you will, Superintendent.'

'Just plain Mr, these days.'

'Yes. Or you wouldn't be here, would you?'

She had her anxieties as rigorously tamed as her cushions.

'Don't worry. I shall not embarrass you by breaking down.'

She wanted her husband back; or else her solicitor, presumably, would not have called out Kenworthy. But there was no suggestion that she was pining for him; no slippers, as it were, in the hearth. Were men's slippers these days ever kept waiting warm for the end of the day's work? Kenworthy's always had been. But Everard's pipe rack, bracketed to the wall by his armchair, had been cleaned and wax-polished. It was oak-carved, with the crest of a Cambridge college. Had her first act, the moment his disappearance was established, been to put his briars out of sight? She must have detested them.

'If you wouldn't mind beginning at the beginning. Just describe in what circumstances you last saw him.'

And that was easy for her: a prepared piece. She sat back, half closed her eyes, and the words flowed out of her.

'Last Tuesday. He left for college in the normal way—that's the Warnford Sixth Form College. There's a lot of private study in the timetable and the place works, both for staff and pupils, on flexi-time. John wasn't

wanted till ten, so he was going along to the surgery to
renew his supply of drugs. Did Mr Hellebore tell you?'

'I'd like to hear it from you, please.'

She had the iron-bound control of a woman who is not
sighing inwardly.

'Seven years ago he had a coronary—not a very massive
one. But he was off work for six months, and has had to
be vigilant since. He is on a low-cholesterol diet, but as
long as he does not miss out on his medicines or overexert
himself physically, he can continue to lead a useful life.'

His regime, the prognosis, did not seem to be subject to
doubt or anxiety.

'At half past ten, the headmaster's secretary rang. He
had not turned up for his Open Scholarship French sem-
inar. Was all well? I rang the surgery, and he had not
been there either. In fact he had called there last Friday
and collected a month's provision.'

'Without mentioning it to you?'

'Obviously without mentioning it to me—otherwise I
would have known about it, would I not? And yet he normally tells me everything. We have always been close, Mr
Kenworthy.'

'Did he leave the house on foot or by car?'

'On foot. He only used the car to college on filthy days.
He is supposed to take exercise, especially walking. And
that is about the only walking he ever does.'

'Had he a case with him?'

'Only his slim briefcase. But there is a suitcase missing
from upstairs. And a basic outfit from his wardrobe:
three of everything—one on, one spare, and one to be
serviced.'

'So he must have succeeded in doing his packing at
some time when you did not know what he was up to.'

There was a rudimentary pause; but she continued
without eruption.

'It must have been on Saturday afternoon. I was invited

to tea by people for whom he does not care: not that that puts them in a minority.'

Kenworthy did not react to the bait of incipient bitterness.

'Then, by the Tuesday afternoon post, *this* came—'

She went to the bureau for a letter of which Kenworthy had already seen a photocopy in the solicitor's office: a fact which he did not reveal now.

Darling:
  CRÈVE-CŒUR:
  No heartaches, please, and no second thoughts. That is why we decided to do things this way.
  Life has been good—and I need not remind you of all those things for which I am inexpressibly grateful.
  But the signs are not to be mistaken: hence CRÈVE-CŒUR.
  There is a blue folder in the second pigeonhole, in which I hope I have left our affairs in good order. The settlement is as generous as I can make it. I do not think I have taken an unfair share for myself.
  Thank you for many things. And don't, please, distress either of us by trying to come after me.

'*Crève-cœur* is the French for heartbreak,' Mrs Everard said.

'Thank you. It also seems to be a code name for a course of action agreed between you.'

'Not between us, Mr Kenworthy. Agreed between my husband and himself, if you like. He would be entitled to expect me to understand the term—not to agree to it. I must make it plain to you as a preliminary to all else that John is an incurable romantic—that is, of course, in the literary, the aesthetic sense.'

'And Operation *Crève-Cœur*?'

'For some years before he had the thrombosis, he suf-

fered from angina. It was entirely his own fault that he
had nothing done about it. He kept insisting that it was
indigestion. He suffers whenever he oversteps the mark,
but controls it with little white tablets that he slips under
his tongue when he feels an attack coming on.'

'Glyceril trinitrate.'

'He has always said that there would come a time when
it would get incurably worse—and he wasn't going to lay
himself up and coddle himself for the rest of his days. He
was not going to be a slow, lingering invalid. He was
going to say a quiet goodbye and vanish into the world:
what he called living it up. If he was going to die, he'd die
enjoying himself. I'd have thought he was joking, but he
had an air of horrible seriousness about him. That was
Operation *Crève-Cœur*.'

She opened her eyes wide and looked at Kenworthy
with her brows raised, as if inviting him to read her mind.

'And fascinated as I am by the prospect of John living it
up, I would greatly prefer to have him here, being
properly looked after and leading a quiet life within his
capacity. Our GP assures me that he could live another
twenty years with common sense and self-control.'

'You haven't yourself been aware of any deterioration
in his condition?'

'He told me ten days ago that he had had to step up his
consumption of trinitrate: two or three tablets a day, instead of his normal three or four a week.'

'So perhaps he had reason to feel concerned about
himself?'

'He has only to follow the simple rules he has been
given; and not allow himself to get unnecessarily worked
up.'

'Worked up about what?'

'Oh, about college; about administrative changes.
About discipline and curriculum and staff meetings.'

'He takes life seriously?'

'He has always been unable to learn what I have been telling him for years: to get on with his job and put it behind him when he comes home—and keep out of college politics.'

'He belonged to the old school, in fact?'

'There was no reason why he should not have continued to do so. He has lost all his chances of promotion. Someone else is headmaster, and he must content himself with running an efficient department. He has never done less than that.'

'May I see the blue folder, please?'

It was an admirably orderly statement of affairs: an analysis of their joint bank account, in which the final balance of £2,091.64 was entirely at her disposal. He would, he said, be drawing no more cheques on it himself, and as token of his intention enclosed his chequebook and bank card. He had left his affairs tidy. Most of the credit balance came from transfers from a deposit account at the same bank, from withdrawals from a building society and from the surrender of a life insurance policy which still had a few years to mature. All major commitments in the immediate future had been cleared: telephone, electricity and half-yearly rates. There was a list of banker's orders and of minor liabilities falling due within the next month: a book club account, a subscription to his professional association; she ought to keep that up in case she ever had to throw herself upon their charity. Finally there was a memorandum telling her exactly how to claim her teacher's widow's pension, when his death should eventually be proven: his reference number, and the address at the Department of Education to which she should write, with a calculation of her expectations in the way of lump sum and monthly payments.

'A systematic man,' Kenworthy said.

'Very.'

Spoken as if she hated him for it.

'And you have a little over £2,000 with which to face the next few months?'

'Is it your fee you are worried about?' Her tongue seemed to get out of control rather easily.

'Not at all,' Kenworthy said silkily. 'I am by no means certain that I ought to saddle myself with your case. I never had the slightest intention, you know, of going into the private agency business. It's just that your solicitor, knowing of my retirement, phoned me to see if I might be interested. And I have come to see whether I am.'

'I'm sorry. I didn't mean—'

He forgave her with a smile and a gesture. He knew, he was suggesting, that she had been under understandable strain.

'I have a few hundreds saved in my own right,' she said. 'And two grown-up children who might perhaps spare me the odd crust if they found me actually starving.'

'He has thought this out down to the finest detail,' Kenworthy said. 'The only point on which I would fault him is over that insurance policy. He's lost heavily there. These people are not noted for the generosity of their surrender values.'

'No. You see, this was a policy that he took out as collateral security when we bought this house, about seventeen years ago. We had a small legacy and paid off the mortgage with it. That freed the policy.'

'So he has wandered off with how much in his pocket, Mrs Everard? Have you tried to work it out?'

She had: she answered readily.

'About eight hundred pounds—plus a five-pound note or two that he might have had in his pocket.'

'Which means that he left you more than half, even of what he got from the policy.'

'He was a very fair-minded man, Mr Kenworthy— about money matters.'

'And pretty well convinced, I would say, that he had not much longer to live.'

'I would have thought that half an hour with his doctor was the sensible step to take about that.'

'Oh, I don't know,' Kenworthy said, and she looked at him sharply, as if she thought he was mocking her. But he went on again in a brisk and friendly manner. She did not know where she stood with him.

'So where do you think he has gone?'

She tightened her lips.

'And please don't tell me,' he said, 'that if you knew the answer to that, you wouldn't be asking to employ me.'

She thought better of several ripostes simultaneously, forced an unnatural relaxation on herself.

'Somewhere on a train,' she said, not bothering to mask underlying derision.

'I scent something positive.'

'I told you that he was a romantic. Trains were all part of it. I don't mean he collected engine numbers or knew about signalling systems. But I've known him go out of his way to be on Liverpool Street Station to watch the night boat-train for Hook of Holland go out. I sometimes think that he read modern languages at Cambridge so that he could travel on the *Rheingold* and go hurtling across France in the middle of the night with the sparks flying.'

'Which train has he gone on this time, do you think? Hook Night?'

'Very probably.'

'And what do you think lies at the end of the track?'

'More track.'

'No woman? You will understand that I have to ask—'

She laughed.

'Mr Kenworthy—I did my best to suggest just now that he is not that kind of romantic.'

She waited for him to go on, but he out-waited her.

'There have been two very high-minded women in his life. I don't regard either of them as a threat. He may have decided to drop in on one or the other of them or both. And it wouldn't distress me if he did. I could hardly wish him anywhere safer.'

Self-delusion? Childish sarcasm? Self-persuasion—with indifferent success?

'Tell me,' Kenworthy said.

'During the war, and for some months afterwards, he was in Field Security.'

Kenworthy stirred, barely perceptibly.

'North West Europe?'

She nodded.

'So was I.'

A light of real hope, the first true sign of it he had seen, came momentarily into her eyes.

'Did you know him?'

'No. But there's nothing unusual in that. We were thin on the ground. And pretty busy.'

'Busy? Yes, I suppose that some of you were. John never told me much working detail. He seems to have got himself fairly well organized—in a non-flamboyant way. He found himself a German lady-friend, a few weeks after the war ended, set her up in a flat; kept her supplied with cigarettes, chocolate and bully beef.'

'He told you about her?'

'He was perfectly frank. He had to get it off his chest as soon as he came home.'

And what had that earned him? Her sympathy? Disappointment and disgust? Or strategically prolonged contempt?

'Where was this?'

'In Schleswig-Holstein. Somewhere up on the North Sea coast. The name of the place will come back to me in a moment.'

'And has he stayed in touch with the lady?'

'They corresponded. Every three months or so for the first few years. Then it dwindled to Christmastime, finally petered out. She wrote him long letters at first—intense, soulful. But no, I don't mean personal. Deep analysis of the moral guilt of the German nation: that kind of thing.'

'You read and speak German yourself, do you?'

'Not a word.'

She twisted her lips self-deprecatingly.

'But he always told me roughly what she'd said.'

'And did he seem involved in her feelings?'

'He took an interest. He always wrote back at similar length.'

Again her curious twisted smile.

'Not that I'm suggesting that their common ground in 1945 and 1946 was entirely philosophical.'

'But you never felt threatened by it?'

'With a man such as John you didn't have to feel threatened by a thing like that. He was too transparent. Of course, I could have wished that it hadn't happened. But I tried to tell myself, they were unnatural times. He came out of the war unscratched—and the odds against that had sometimes seemed astronomical. Husum: that's the name of the place.'

'And the lady's name?'

'Lieselotte Mölling. A war widow.'

And how had Mrs Everard taken the revelation in fact? With the patient resignation that she implied? Or with that stiff-necked martyrdom that went with her physical appearance now? Had his reward for his transparency been weeks of estrangement from her, satisfying her puritanical narcissicism? Or had she not been beyond using his conscience as a lash for prolonged marital blackmail?

And what, if anything, had John Everard learned from Lieselotte Mölling? Anything that had affected his subsequent performances with his wife? If she was a woman to notice such things—

Some of the German women of that generation, Kenworthy remembered, their men lost, their hope of men

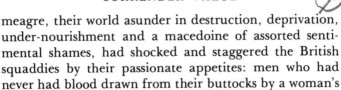

meagre, their world asunder in destruction, deprivation, under-nourishment and a macedoine of assorted sentimental shames, had shocked and staggered the British squaddies by their passionate appetites: men who had never had blood drawn from their buttocks by a woman's fingernails before.

'When were you married?' Kenworthy asked inconsequentially.

'1943.'

'And when was your first child born?'

'1948.'

'And has your husband ever met Frau Mölling since?'

'No.'

'He has been back to Germany?'

'Many times — but never to the north. Always the Rhine Valley, Bavaria or the Black Forest.'

'With you?'

'He was usually in charge of school parties. I hardly ever went with him.'

'Then there was nothing to prevent her travelling cross-country to meet him?'

'I would have known. He would have told me. His conscience was too tender to be true.'

Which had earned him only her contempt?

'Have you anything else to tell me, Mrs Everard?'

'There was a woman in France that people used to pull his leg about.'

'With any justification?'

'I think not. I'm sure not. I met her once, and it was purely an intellectual friendship.'

'And what period of his life did that cover?'

'The last fifteen years.'

'A fair slice.'

She brushed it aside with the visible and outward signs of a mental shudder.

'Let's not inflate it out of proportion. I'm telling you

about it because you clearly have to know everything. But
you're wasting your time if you think the trail will lead
you anywhere.'

'But do fill me in, please.'

'Ever since he took charge of modern languages here in
Warnford, he has put hours of his own time into organizing foreign travel for his pupils. He built himself a sort of
axis with Caudebec en Caux, in Normandy — Madame
Bovary's town. He had a network of families who would
take in children as paying guests. He laid on excursions,
liaised with local schools, fixed up tennis, basketball,
country walks, folk song evenings — '

'You used to go with him?'

'Once only. It was no sort of holiday for me. He was so
tied up with his problems: homesickness, children who
wouldn't eat French food, bed-wetters, laying clues for
childish treasure hunts about the countryside.'

'And his lady-friend?'

'You're getting the wrong impression. It was always
work first with John Everard. And work made more work,
as you can imagine. It's a wonder he found time at all for
Marie-Thérèse Besson.'

'Who was — *is* — she?'

'Who knows? She's supposed to have some vague aristo-
cratic connection. I'll settle for the vagueness. She lives in
a house standing on its own on a hillside overlooking the
Seine. And she fancies herself: elaborate hairstyle, a ring
for every finger, but her window frames are rotting for a
coat of paint. Antique furniture — monumental, polished
like something sacred. But needs notice if there's to be
any demand on the larder.'

'What age?'

'When I met her — that would be about twelve years
ago — she was doing her best to look *our* age.'

Kenworthy, Everard, Everard's wife, Lieselotte Mölling, Marie-Thérèse Besson: they all belonged in the same pocket of history.

'How did your husband meet her?'

'Through the local mayor, when he was making his initial arrangements.'

'And you think he was quite fond of her?'

'He liked her company. He sometimes went up in the evening to talk to her. He usually seemed to have one tête-à-tête supper with her on each of his visits. They used to talk existentialism when it was all the vogue: Sartre and Kierkegaard. They had a thing about a man called Heidegger.'

'At least you've been able to keep up with your modern philosophy.'

'What, me? Do I look like a philosopher? Making ends meet on the Burnham Scale, that's been my lot.'

'But it was all part of your husband's work, wasn't it? If he was dealing with university entrants, it would be of great value to him, wouldn't it, having this contact with ideas across the Channel?'

'I dare say. I know they swopped the *Observer* and *Figaro*. I didn't begrudge him that.'

'Did they correspond much?'

'Sporadically. She was useful to him as a contact on the ground — helped him to find billets for his students — to place vegetarians in suitable houses — that kind of thing.'

'Otherwise — ?'

'Otherwise I am quite sure there was nothing between them. What drew attention to her was that she became a bit of a joke with the children who went out with his parties; even with some of the colleagues who helped him out: John Everard and his lady-love up on the hill. There was even a veiled reference to her once in the school magazine. That upset him very much indeed.'

'And yet you don't feel that —'

'I am as certain as I can be of anything that Madame

Besson meant nothing to him beyond a well-sited human machine who talked and thought in French.'

'You think it's unlikely that he's gone to see her on his present travels?'

'I wouldn't like to say for sure.'

She averted her eyes, then remembered to bring them back to Kenworthy's face.

'If he really thinks he hasn't long to live, do you not think he might have gone to say a sort of goodbye in Germany and France? Is he sentimental enough for that?'

'Every bit sentimental enough.'

And when had his wife last stirred sentiment in him?

'But you'd hardly call that living it up, would you?' Kenworthy asked. 'You've drawn me a portrait, Mrs Everard, of a man puritan by temperament.'

'That would be a fair description of him.'

More puritan than thou. But Kenworthy did not frame the thought.

'I think he may have had inflated notions about the lusts and fleshpots of the carefree,' she said.

'Has he ever shown the slightest inclination in the direction of the fleshpots? When the barriers are down, the puritans often turn out to be the worst whole-hoggers of the lot—or so I'm told.'

'I can't imagine it of John.'

'So whatever gaudy sins he may have dreamed of in his secret moments—you think he might fight shy of them at the moment of confrontation—even if he knew where to start looking for them?'

'He'd be more likely to kill himself on the outward journey, trying to carry a suitcase too heavy for him. If he's in the state he thinks he's in, he ought to be in an intensive care unit, Mr Kenworthy.'

'People sometimes die in intensive care units. Maybe that's just what he wants to avoid.'

'He might have shown a little consideration for me.'

Kenworthy allowed a silence to develop amid the in-hospitable tidiness — only for seconds: long enough for a clock to be ticking, a rose tendril to rustle in the garden, for street noises — a milkman's electric float, an infant on a tricycle, a two-tone door chime — to penetrate in muffled fashion from the world outside.

'I'm afraid I've been what the lawyers call leading you, Mrs Everard. Bad practice. An inefficient way to conduct an interview. The decadence of retirement, probably. Where do you think he's gone?'

'If I knew the answer to that, Mr Kenworthy, I wouldn't have —'

'I don't mean anything you'd have thought of reporting to the local inspector. I mean something vaguer than that — much vaguer; something vague but persistent, perhaps.'

She went through the motions of thinking about it — though she gave the inescapable impression that she could have picked it up immediately from very close under the surface.

'Without evidence, Mr Kenworthy — without any kind of evidence — it sounds silly even to mention it.'

He waited.

'A few years ago, we went to Austria. The Tirol — the Zillertal. The first time we'd been away together without our children — the first time for ages that John had been away without a flock of other people's children. To be honest, I didn't enjoy the trip. We ate too much and I don't like mountains. I did my best not to spoil it for John — I'm being brutally frank with you, Mr Kenworthy — brutally frank with myself, too. I could not begin to feel about the place as John did. When we went for coach trips up the Alpine valleys, I felt physically sick every time I looked out of the window. I don't care for sit-ting in smoky atmospheres staring at great stone pots of beer. I don't like phoney folk music, with all that touristic yodelling and blaring brass.'

'And John did?'

'He knew it was spurious, but he got pleasure out of it. He said he knew it was an illusion — but a satisfying one. Don't worry: I am coming to the point. And let me say again: I've no reason to think this: it's a sort of vision. No: that's putting it too strongly — it's a picture; something that keeps coming back into my mind. We went one day by the post-bus up into the mountains. I can't for the life of me tell you where. I've lost track of dates, times and places. And there was a footpath that went up by a rivulet — up, up and up — up a rocky pass — and you kept seeing the summit round the next hairpin — until you got there. And then there it was, towering above you again, as far away as ever. If you went far enough, that footpath went on into Italy. I don't know how far: there must have been a frontier post over the crest. It was all terribly arid, a gorge strewn with rocks, and lesser gorges opening up from it: cold mountain streams. It didn't strike me that Italy was likely to look any different from Austria.'

There was a fluency about her now, as if it was not the first time that she had expressed these thoughts.

'You'll say I've no poetry in me — well, maybe I haven't — not that kind of poetry. But I knew it was very different for John. It was something he'd never grown out of. There's always been a magic in strange places for him; even if it's a magic that he makes up about them himself. Here was a footpath that led over a mountain pass into Italy: a country, as it happened, that he'd never set foot in. I told you just now how he felt about trains. Trains were magic because they went to strange places. You know, I may sound cold and casual about it, but I can see how it was with him. As a boy he'd been to a small country grammar school. Even beginning to learn French had seemed an adventure. Getting to France — even getting to London from his provincial corner — was a voyage of discovery. And now he found himself on a rocky footpath to Italy.'

The milkman rattled bottles on the Everards' doorstep.

'So I told him that if he was thinking of walking into Italy, that was all right with me; but I was going to sit where I was and wait till he got back. I wasn't nasty about it, you understand; it was a fact of my life. I had a paperback in my bag, a Georgette Heyer, and the sun was shining — though the wind was on the sharp side for August. I sat on a pile of stones, and I waited.'

'Just a moment: was this before or after his thrombosis?'

'You are wondering how he could cope with that climb in spite of his angina? It was *after*: about a year after his convalescence. He could walk quite long distances, manage quite steep gradients — once he'd got going — provided he'd got his pills with him — and as long as the weather wasn't too cold. Also — and when I say this, don't think I'm getting at him — a lot depended on the frame of mind he was in. Anyway, he was gone over an hour. And when he came back, he was fairly bursting with health: and most apologetic. He hadn't got to the frontier, hadn't even reached the top of the pass. There'd always been that new upward stretch after the next hairpin. And he'd turned back, not because the exertion was getting too much for him, but because he was worried about me, alone on those rocks all that time. He was worried about me because he thought I'd be worrying about him.'

She was flushed by the vigour that she had put into the telling of it. 'I was annoyed with him, I admit — unjustly perhaps. If he'd kept me waiting there much longer, I'd probably have been angrier still. I was uncomfortable, the afternoon was getting definitely chilly, and if he'd actually gone on into his precious Italy, it would probably have been getting dark by the time he got back. And it all seemed so futile — all that effort on his part, all that hanging about on mine—and nothing achieved. As far as I could make out, he hadn't even seen Italy—or, and this was the most idiotic thing about it, he didn't know for certain whether he had or not. That was the colour of his whole life. That was how I used to feel when he was putting in for headmasterships. He had so much in his favour—on paper; but he could never swing a committee into voting for him. He always came back from his interviews with the same look that he brought down from that Austrian mountain: resignation to failure. But afterwards, he often spoke of that afternoon above the Zillertal. He always said that one day he would go back and finish that walk.'

Kenworthy altered his posture, clasped his fingers under his chin and looked at her with a penetration that might or might not have been sympathetic.

'So you think that's where he might have gone now?'

'It would be typical.'

Kenworthy stood up and went and looked, more than casually, at the titles in the bookcase. But he came back to his chair without following up any idea that they might have given him.

'Let us stop shadow-boxing, Mrs Everard. We know there is one angle that we have both been avoiding.'

She looked at him tensely, admitting nothing.

'It may well be a coincidence that a sixteen-year-old girl, one of his own students, should have disappeared on the same day that he did.'

She maintained her tension, primly controlling her speech.

'As you say: a coincidence.'

'It is being suggested that she had an adolescent crush on him.'

'He is far too experienced a schoolmaster to allow himself to be affected by that.'

'Sometimes even the most prudent of men finds himself flattered by such a state of affairs.'

'Not John. I have heard him talk objectively about this situation when it has happened to others.'

'You are very sure of him.'

'Very sure.'

'Even if he had decided on an uncharacteristic last fling?'

'Even if that were true. He is too professional. His professionalism goes deeper into his bones than anything else about him.'

'I would like to think you are right.'

'Even if it had crossed his mind to go off with this girl, he would never allow a situation to develop that might harm her.'

Kenworthy looked again towards Everard's academic library.

'How many of those have you read?'

'None. They are not in my line. I am no sort of linguist.'

He uncrossed his legs, getting ready to rise from his chair.

'There's one thing that puzzles me, Mrs Everard.'

'There are a number of things that puzzle me.'

'One thing above all others: what do you want him back *for*?'

CHAPTER 3

When the man who had signed himself Joseph Kite left the Ambassadeurs hotel, he took his young lady-friend—who was not even walking close to him—for a desultory walk round the town. Mostly they contented themselves with looking in shop-windows and sometimes, if the display did not interest her, the girl stood some distance away from the man, her back turned towards him. They made one purchase each, at a small stationer's: he bought an Ordnance Survey map of the North Norfolk coast. She spent a little time choosing a rather tasteless comic birthday card, at which he appeared to remonstrate with her. Not only did the card seem to displease him, but he insisted that she give it to him, which she did with ill grace. He put it away in an inside pocket.

Eventually they made their way past upturned boats, past kiosks lashed-up for the off-season. On the beach a middle-aged woman, her royal-blue slacks tight against her fat thighs, was throwing the remains of a flotsam sandal into the surf for the amusement of a boisterous dog. She was smoking a cigarette as she threw.

The patent turnstile of the early-century pier stood open, but the mark that lay over everything was a sort of non-nostalgia for the departed season. A carpenter called Walter Fothergill, who was measuring up broken timbers in the children's helter-skelter, watched them go past the tattooist's gallery, the padlocked T-shirt stall and an abandoned bar, towards the furthest extremity of the jetty. And it was as they were approaching the last rail that Gypsy Rosanna came out of her cabin and emptied a teapot into the sea. She was a fleshless woman, with no hint of the clairvoyant in her appearance, with a faded kerchief over her head, and wearing a brown coat so drab that one wondered why it had attracted her when it was new.

Inside the window of her booth she had sellotaped typewritten testimonials from various Germanic-sounding aristocrats, and these seemed to interest the weary, pale girl. This time it was her companion's turn to remain a few paces apart, as if the exhibition was beneath his contempt. Returning with her empty teapot, Gypsy Rosanna recognized the meaning in the girl's eyes—an interest which she could not quite bring herself to express—and asked her if she wanted to come in. The girl said something to her escort, which Walter Fothergill was too far away to catch, but which appeared to be a hangdog request for permission. The man shrugged his shoulders, looked at his watch and walked a symbolic couple of paces further away; which the girl seemed to interpret as curmudgeonly agreement, for she went through the door that Rosie-Anne held open for her.

In a West Country market town the landlady who had the previous afternoon turned a couple away opened her front door to set the clock finger on the dial which gave orders to her milkman. And she caught sight of the couple again, the man looking even more dejected than yesterday, the girl even more of a brazen tart.

So somebody must have given them a bed for the night.

'And I said to myself, that will be Lorna Bell over on Lismore Terrace. Some people might be a bit more thoughtful if they had daughters of their own.'

There seemed something unlovably efficient about the man who stood beyond the ticket barrier, scanning the boat-train that was discharging its passengers like a defecating python. Evidently he was here to meet a stranger, for he referred more than once to a snapshot that he had palmed away in his hand.

Then he spotted her, and put the photograph away in his pen-pocket. There looked nothing of the stranger-in-a-lonely-land about the girl whom he went forward to meet. She was a Spaniard and had made firm friends on her journey—with two young men with guitars on their shoulders—and they seemed in no hurry to take their leave of her.

The gentleman worked his way over to her through the crowd and put his fingers round the handle of her suitcase. She stepped back, looked into his face—and bolted.

She left him holding her case and shot off diagonally, ploughing through a party of nuns who were being shepherded by an improbably young-looking cleric. By the time that her would-be mentor had made his way decorously round the tail of this crocodile, the Spanish girl was nowhere in sight.

The ticket-collector — who would not have remembered the girl but for the hilarious adroitness of her flight — was not in a position to say whether her escort caught up with her or not.

Meanwhile, on a rack in a back room in a police station near Euston Square, another suitcase was gathering dust. It contained the clothes of an adolescent girl, and a few uninviting literary texts. No one had been to claim it.

CHAPTER 4

Kenworthy came back along the Avenue, serenely undistressed by the scene that he had loosed off.

But one thing above all others: what do you want him back for?

Blanche Everard had played fragments of various roles during the interview, but her fury over this sleepy-sounding piece of insolence had been genuine. So it was the images that mattered — both the public and the private one: the showcase of a stable, 'loving' marriage.

And, of course, it must be shown to the world that her husband had not run away with this Shires girl.

Kenworthy sat with provocation unrepentantly fixed on his face. And, of course, she climbed down.

'I'm afraid you've got the wrong impression, Mr Kenworthy. But then, if you're not *interested* —'

'Oh — I am *interested.*'

'You will find him for us?'

For *us* — their most darling possession —

'I am tempted to look for him. But I am far from convinced that that would be playing fair. I would not be in a position, you know, to bring any pressure to bear on him.'

'I don't understand, Mr Kenworthy. I would have thought—'

'It's his own decision. It seems to me that he's thought it out pretty carefully. And he's left you in at least as sound a financial position as you would be if he retired on a breakdown pension — bar about eight hundred pounds that he proposes to blue.'

'But surely, to get him under proper medical attention—'

'Medical science, Mrs Everard, is paying increasing attention to setting the scene for a man to die.'

'I am not convinced that my husband is as sick as all that.'

'But you cannot be sure.'

'Then I have the right to make sure. You men do like to stick together, don't you?'

'I haven't said no yet, Mrs Everard.'

He walked back along the Avenue, past a Television Rental service van and a salesman checking his order book in a parked Allegro. And so he reached the High Street, Warnford: a market town that had retained something of its rural provenance, a commuter's hour from London. He entered the overlapping squares of a small shopping precinct: a card shop, a wine store, an Oxfam shopwindow. He made a beeline for a tobacconist's of the old-fashioned sort, displaying little bowls of what the proprietor claimed to be his own flakes and mixtures. He had to wait his turn behind a tall, sulky yet confident young man who was trying to sell rather than buy.

The proprietor was a piggy-eyed, dapper and bad-

tempered man who favoured short-back-and-sides, a
heavy moustache and a dark suit, and who was aggress-
ively not interested in what was being offered to him. The
youngster, who would be eighteen or nineteen, was untroubled by initial opposition.

'You can have them on sale or return, with a fifteen per
cent rake-off. And we wondered whether you'd care to
take advertisement space in the next issue: five quid a
quarter page, or fifteen quid for a month's run. I might
say our next number is likely to cause a stir. We're treb-
ling the run.'

'You can take that bloody rubbish out of this shop. And
if you want my advice, you'll put the whole bloody printing straight in an old sack for salvage.'

The boy shrugged his shoulders in what might possibly
have been a nervous tic. He was clean-looking about face
and hands, dressed in Levis with a heavy Aran sweater
and had in his eyes a kind of complacent intelligence. His
shoulders drooped slightly and some observers would have
diagnosed a tendency to outgrow his strength.

'I hope you won't regret it,' he said. 'We do have other
outlets. And as I've said, next week's number is likely to
be in some demand. We might even run to a supplement-
ary this week.'

'What is it you're selling?'

Kenworthy spoke, and the youngster turned and looked
at him with a habit of languid insolence, too wrapped up
in himself to take notice of other people's personalities.
He had under his arm a sheaf of cyclostyled sheets, a
private newspaper, stapled together in folios of four or
five pages.

'Fifteen pence, sir. Can I interest you?'

Kenworthy brought out small change, folded the document twice and put it away in an inner pocket without
looking at it. The boy walked past him out of the shop,
his shoulders twitching as he went through the door.

'I'll have a two-ounce tin of Mick M'Quaid, if I may.'

'And a very wise man you're going to be,' the tobacconist said, 'when you've digested that load of crap.'

'Something from the college, I suppose.'

The man leaned across his counter as if he saw in Kenworthy something of a soul-mate: ex-serviceman, reactionary and hankerer after good old days in which they had both been prime grumblers.

'College, did you say? College? Six hundred bloody idlers whose sole purpose is to provide employment for a staff of so-called graduates—and to provide an income for a café that that police ought to shut down? Two bloody years—three, in some cases—on what they call flexitime—to take A-level in one bloody subject: Art? Listen, old friend, *I'm* an old boy of that school. Well—let's not be blasphemous: of what used to be Warnford Grammar School. When it *was* a school. When you got four across your arse if you were seen eating an ice-cream in the street. And if you were wearing your cap at the time, you got two more for bringing it into disrepute. And if you weren't wearing your cap, that was two for not wearing it.'

'Aye,' Kenworthy said.

'Now they can come down the High Street smoking with their hands in their pockets. And I wouldn't mind so much if it was only tobacco. Would you mind very much if I just took a squint at that rubbish you just bought?'

Kenworthy brought out the paper, which the man unfolded and put on the counter, smoothing out the paper with stubby, well-manicured fingers.

'Yes. I thought as much. They're pouring fuel on that smouldering heap.'

He had found a column which, Kenworthy read upside down, was headed STOP PRESS.

'*Cause célèbre?*' he asked hopefully.

'You might say that. One of the masters up there has

chucked a dummy. Had enough of it. Napoo. And I can't say I blame him. Nice chap—one of the old-timers. Comes in here twice a week for an ounce of *John Cotton*, which of itself puts him down as a gentleman of breeding. We always have a chat, same as I'm talking to you. He's never been one to complain a lot, but by God you could see what he was up against: headmaster who doesn't know whether his arsehole is punched, bored or counter-sunk—and who'll back a pupil against a member of staff any time of night or day. They talk about pupil power: it isn't pupil power we're up against, if you ask me, it's sheer bloody weakness of those we are paying to keep things on an even keel. Anyway, this fellow Everard: nice bloke; he's taken off. Gone walkabout. Not a trace. Not the echo of a fart. Took the London train, and that's the beginning and end of it. Has a bit of a dicky heart into the bargain, just to worry his folks a bit more. But I'll tell you what, my old China, I'm not surprised. You'd only to look at John Everard these last few weeks to know he was heading for a breakdown.'

The tobacconist read for a few seconds.

'What is more, the same day that Everard went, a lass from one of the top forms decides that she's ready for a bit of a change as well. She'd been asked for an interview at a training college on the outskirts of London—and never been seen since. It doesn't take much of a Sherlock for some people to decide that they must have travelled on the same train.'

He looked up from the duplicated sheet with his black little eyes flashing.

'So two and two have been put together, making x squared plus y squared, and this town is split into two factions, one half of which believes that Mr Everard and Miss Shires have gone out into the sticks together.'

Kenworthy began to laugh, whereupon the tobacconist looked up with an unexpressed question.

'Mathematically speaking, two plus two could be expressed as x squared plus y squared,' he said pleasantly, 'if x equals y, for example.'

'Not in this bloody case.'

'You seem very sure of that.'

'Because I know both parties.'

'Ah.'

'The Shires. Really nice people. Lived here all their lives. I've known Sue's mother since she was so high. And that child has been brought up as a child should be. No side. And none of your hard rock. You'll not see her in jeans. Or without a little crucifix round her neck.'

Kenworthy did not argue any point.

'Not the sort to go running off with a man in his fifties,' he suggested.

The tobacconist pulled a serio-comic face.

'Who'd go running off with you or me?' he said.

'Who indeed?'

'And friend Everard least of all. A man whose middle name is propriety. A man who lives only for his job—or did, while there was still hope of being allowed to do it properly.'

The shop-keeper looked up from the news-sheet, and Kenworthy turned it round on the counter so that he could do justice to it himself.

There was a good deal of teenage esoterica:

WE WOULD LIKE TO KNOW—

Who left the lights burning all night in E2?

Who thought that a Sylph was a disease that can be cured by antibiotics?

On the second half of the same page was the item that mattered:

STOP PRESS

Far be it from us to risk baking under a lawyer's crust by referring to a matter that is sub judice. But is it or isn't it? Let us, to quote a comment not infrequently seen gracing the margins of our history essays, Be

Precise. Or, to reduce the issue to that Christmas-cracker world in which some of our appointed leaders seem to live and move and have their being, when is sub judice *not* sub judice?

We remain unconvinced that the lamented disappearance of the erstwhile so prudent Eduardo and the once-exemplary Shires Filly is being taken with sufficient seriousness by those who (as we have been confidently told by one of them) are their best hope of redemption.

We on the staff of The Collegian *do not believe that E. and S. have gone their separate ways. Why will officialdom not admit the outstanding probability that somewhere in our green and pleasant land the pair may at this moment be attempting a clear round in double harness? Or may they not have undertaken a picturesque train-ride to some Ultima Thule where French or German is the operative tongue?*

There are some who would maintain that we ought not to make this our business; that if ever a couple unequivocally needed each other, Ed and Sue do. But is this good enough? Might not Sue stand in need of protection from that look that is seen in Ed's eyes when sly mention is made of the charmer of Caudebec? And as for Ed: could we be callous enough to leave him defenceless against the smouldering fires that his young supporter has heretofore reserved for reverend young gentlemen in full canonicals?

We believe that we on The Collegian *have information that is being neglected by those charged with the exploration of this veritable ghetto of Avenues. We believe that our evidence is being ignored in a world where more is sometimes known in the Copa Cabana than by Central Criminal Records.*

We therefore propose to take certain matters into our own hands, to follow up for ourselves certain threads in the labyrinth; assuring, of course, our unstinted co-operation if proper regard is paid to it.

Watch, therefore, this column for future revelations. Watch, even, for extraordinary editions of this organ.

We feel it our duty to step in where the failure of others seems certain. We shall supplement the age-weary experience of the Establishment with our pristine presence at the fount of events. If we do not do this, which of us, teacher or taught, catechist or catechumen, can be free of the fear of abduction? We shall not feel safe at nights, either in or between beds.

'Clever stuff,' Kenworthy said. 'And how thoroughly bloody nasty!'

'Those bastards up there have made Everard's life hell. Not that he's ever said so in so many words, but I've been reading between the lines for months now—for years, in fact, ever since this new place went up. The poor devil just wasn't moulded to teach in a so-called permissive society.'

'This Copa Cabana—that'll be the café you mentioned just now?'

'Yes. It's practically become a college annexe. Or maybe it's the college that's the annexe.'

'How do I get there?'

CHAPTER 5

The middle-aged, spare and rather convalescent-looking gentleman began to wonder whether his fly-buttons were undone—or if someone had painted obscene graffiti on his back. Even in the comparative haven of the Tolhouse Museum (it was raining heavily in Great Yarmouth) he was aware of a certain curiously studious interest being taken in him by strangers. Even members of the curator's staff left the door of their office ajar and peeped out at intervals at the couple who were wandering dejectedly about the local history exhibits. For the mournful man in the grey gabardine was accompanied by a young lady in the full bloom of metamorphosis into womanhood: perhaps she had overdone her cosmetics a little, and her eyes were not yet conscious of the effect they might have on passing males.

Public interest in John Everard and Susan Shires was now at full bristle. A Warnford reporter, who was also a stringer for a national daily, had got hold of a copy of *The Collegian* and its editorial had crystallized the belief that the pair were at large together. *College Master Betrays Trust* was the sentiment that epitomized the public temper. Consequently, any middle-aged stranger escorting an attractive adolescent of the opposite sex was likely to become the object of loaded judgement.

On a wet day in out-of-season Yarmouth the interest of various unconnected observers led to quick action. As the man and the girl stepped from the Museum into the drizzle, they were approached by a policeman whose panda car was parked a little distance up the road. He was an experienced officer, who preferred a leisurely and oblique approach to unsolicited denunciations and he chatted amicably about the weather, the decline of the herring fisheries and the best bar snacks in town. All this led him to establish — for he was an astute operator — that the man was divorced from his wife and had access to his boarding-schooled daughter this weekend.

At a police station near a London terminus a detective-constable looked across the table from his spread copy of the *Sun* and remembered the nametapes on the underwear in a nearly new suitcase. Within half an hour his inspector was on the phone to Warnford.

At a seasonally prosperous pub on the North Norfolk

coast the man who had once signed himself Joseph
Kite — now alchemized into William Townshend — arrived
with his child-wife at that hour between afternoon closing
and evening opening when it is difficult to discover
whether life as we know it continues to exist about an
English inn. The front door was defiantly bolted, and un-
furnished with either knocker or bell. Even the kitchen
sink, viewed after the navigation of an archipelago of
discarded kegs and crated empties, had about it
something of the air of the *Marie Celeste*, as if the
Coastguard, between Brancaster and Stiffkey, were a
wilful ship found deserted at the edge of the autumn-
blown coastal road.

But as the seekers were about to abandon their quest, a
face appeared at an upper window and a woman's fingers
grappled with a window-fastening. Gladys Turnbull, ro-
tund, menopausal, her hair in its afternoon rollers, looked
out and down and had no doubt whatever about the identity
of the travellers.

Gladys Turnbull, like at least one person's estimate of
John Everard, was an unrepentant romantic, though in
her case her outlook was not limited to the literary or
æsthetic. She was a woman to whom love between the
sexes, young or old, lawful or scandalous, rose-strewn or
star-crossed, was invariably touching. The sight of a couple
absorbed in each other always brought a warm tear hap-
pily close to the corner of her eye; she had been known to
have a comfy little weep over the announcement of an
engagement in a geriatric ward. Gladys Turnbull was
always ready to advance the cause of love whenever she
spotted or thought she spotted it. Sometimes she thought
she had spotted it when its promotion was far from the
desires or convenience of either party, and she had several
times arrived in situations which had exasperated her
husband. But he had long since seen the futility of
remonstration — and retreated into interests of his own.

The one maxim which, she claimed, governed her existence, was that she minded her own business and let other people mind theirs. The neatest summary of her suggestibility is that she truly believed both halves of this to be true. But the policy did at least enable her to ignore official points of view—including the law of the land—whenever these appeared to conflict with the happy sentimental relationships that she saw about her.

Consequently, the appearance of John Everard and Susan Shires at her back door at the slackest hour of the day brought a familiar flutter into her fattily enlarged heart.

'It's lucky for you I'm an old softie,' she said to them as she let them in, which they did not understand. But then there were quite a lot of other remarks that she made to them as she showed them up her crooked staircase that did not appear to have any meaning except to herself. Mrs Turnbull was a woman who expected strangers to be *au fait* with the allusions, even with the secret language, the by-words and catch-phrases of her private existence. She looked at the couple and saw that the man was decent, subdued—and transparently proud of his young bride. The girl she found modest, unspoiled by the garish age in which she lived—and perhaps just a little embarrassed by having her innermost susceptibilities read by a pageant of strangers; everything she saw in her, Gladys Turnbull put down very strongly in her favour. She mentally christened the girl Rosebud, secretly comparing her with an ephemeral blossom blown in a June hedgerow.

In objective fact, the girl was pale, drawn and pouty. She sat down heavily on the edge of the bed and looked at the man—whose eyes were for the moment not on her—with an expression of time-expired exasperation. And when he said to her something about the view across the saltings, she appeared not to hear him. All of which Gladys Turnbull ascribed to her admirable reticence about parading her intimate feelings in public.

'You'll feel better, ducky, when you've got a good meal inside you.'

But the young woman did not appear at the dinner-table. The man came down, apologetically, alone, saying that she was feeling a little off-colour, and could he have just some light snack to take up to her?

'A light snack?'

Gladys Turnbull was not fluent in the language of poor appetites.

'She says a packet of crisps is all she fancies.'

'A packet of crisps!' Mrs Turnbull could not believe that the young woman knew what she was talking about. 'I'll tell you what I'll do. I'll make up a dainty little tray for you, and I'm sure when she sees it, it will start her juices running.'

She loaded a plate with two lamb chops, of the solidity said to be preferred in the Yorkshire town of Barnsley, four roast potatoes, eight tablespoons of winter cabbage, a mountain of Brussels sprouts and a foothill of mashed swede. It was found unbroached and congealed when the daily woman did out the bedroom next morning.

The Coastguard and its residents passed a strenuous night. The man purporting to be William Townshend spent the inside of the evening in the public bar where, with the encouragement and advice of half a dozen local bait-diggers, he ended up with a credit balance of thirty pence from the fruit-machine. He went up to bed early, oblivious of the ribald prophecies that began before the bar door was safely closed behind him. He appeared to be undisturbed by the comings and goings that made the pub a far more active place at four in the morning than it had been at four in the afternoon. For every other guest in the house — there were five of them, all male — was here for the autumn beach-fishing, a craft which absorbed their talk at the bar and which closely involved the landlord. George Turnbull was more than a devotee; he saw no other reason for existence, and had years ago abandoned any attempt to draw reason from his wife in favour of attracting a cod of *Angling Times* proportions from behind the second line of breakers.

There was therefore an exodus from the Coastguard at a quarter to two in the morning. Men filed out with Tilley-lamps, wicker baskets and rod-bags to catch a propitious tide. The noise they made was prodigious. Though normally, doubtless, considerate men, there was a sanctity about the incoming autumn codling that absolved them from their routine codes and ethical systems. But there was no evidence that they woke William Townshend.

The girl, on the other hand, appeared to have been disturbed by the mass movement. About three-quarters of an hour after the hissing lamps had been deployed by their tripods along the tideline, she let herself out of the inn and crossed the road towards the sandy track that led down to the beach. Although there was a spiteful chill in the night, she had not taken the trouble to dress properly, but had merely thrown a loose jacket — it appeared to be a man's — about her shoulders over her long white nightdress. She was wearing floppy sandals that she had difficulty in keeping on her feet and moved through the fine dry sand with a shuffling gait. The moonlight was cold, sharp and utterly colourless, so that she seemed to glide like a kind of phantom — the sort of apparition that could easily have established an obstinate local legend, if anyone had seen her.

But no one did — at this stage. For fifty yards or so the sandy rutted track was cut off from its flanking dunes by wire fences, but when she came at last to a gap — the wire had been trodden down, and one of its posts uprooted — she crossed it and made her way laboriously up the ridge of one of the sand hills. She was now silhouetted

against the skyline, and if any of the fishermen, in line
abreast on the foreshore some two hundred yards in front
of her, had turned and caught sight of her, the experience might well have affected his attitude to the
supernatural for the rest of his days. Her presence alone
could have struck terror; but there was also something in
her movements that seemed apart from normal human
behaviour—an occasional lifting of her arm away from
her side in a gesture that belonged to classical ballet. And
now and then she tossed her head in exaggerated fashion,
as if freeing her hair to the will of the elements, as if ex-
ulting in some kind of symbolic liberation.

At last she found a pine log to sit on and perched
herself on it with her elbows on her knees, her chin in her
hands, looking out to where the crest of a breaker creamed
open and spilled into the lunar shadows.

It was almost an hour later before the man came out of
the Coastguard. He too had had to dress hurriedly, but he
had at least thrown an adequacy of garments upon himself, though he had not given himself time to button his
raincoat and he walked with the discomfort of a man
whose pyjamas are rucked up inside his trousers. He did
not see the girl at first: as long as she remained still, she
might have been no more than another twisted column of
grotesque driftwood cast high and dry on the dunes. He
walked first in the direction of the fishermen, one or other
of whom turned occasionally to make a cast without paying attention to him. And then the girl caught sight of
him.

Her reaction was to rise sharply to her feet and take a
few steps backwards in the sand, as if even at this distance
silence and stealth must be the order of her day. And
then, suddenly flinging her arms about in uncoordinated
fashion, she turned and ran into the fringe of trees and
tufty grass.

The man turned his head at the critical moment and

spotted the flailing limbs in the white moonlight. At once
he began to run too, a long-limbed, ungainly lope, his
feet slopping first in the wet shingle of the tideline, then
ploughing deep into the clinging dry sand further up the
beach.

With the exception of one man who had at that moment thought he had detected a bite, the eyes of the
anglers were now all on the chase. There was even an
ironical cheer as the man thrust his body forward, pitting
himself against the almost impossible running surface by
willpower; he showed little evidence of athletic training.
The girl, on the other hand, once her back was turned on
her pursuer, seemed to take inspired flight, her nightdress
fluttering behind her calves and her hair now almost
horizontal in her own slipstream. There seemed no
chance at all that the man would catch her.

And yet, five minutes later, they came, together, to the
intersection where the lane turned off from the main
road, opposite the hotel. They were walking slowly now,
his arm about her shoulders and her cheek leaning into
his. Looking out of her bedroom window, a discreet foot
or so behind a camouflage of curtain, Mrs Gladys Turnbull sighed at the infectious happiness of the sight.

In a small town in Hertfordshire, Inspector Pocock scanned
the Crime Report and threw it into the tray for filing
without much hope, without fire — without even interest.
It was a statistic, rather than a call for action.

Ten thousand people a year in the kingdom went missing; it was the fourth time in two years that this one had
gone adrift; the second time, she had been out in the
unknown for ten weeks.

Pocock did his stints at his desk lethargically to the
point of lassitude; he could behave differently when he
spotted something urgent. In this instance he knew,
without having to run his pencil down a check list, that

everything was running according to the book. There was no loophole for comeback here.

Officially, she must rate as an escapee. But she was no danger to the public at large; the only one likely to be in jeopardy was herself—and there wasn't much likelihood of that. The gods had always been on her side; she was a miraculous survivor. There was no justification for intensity of action in a world where there wasn't enough intensity of action to go round. Her description had gone for the fourth time in flimsies to neighbouring stations who would know what to do with them. Next of kin had been informed: not that they cared. Associates? She had never provided evidence that she had any. Relatives? Only the sort she'd stay away from. Indications of intention? Survival, solitude—and then some sudden burst of exhibitionism. There was little need for circulation to other forces at this stage. The *Police Gazette* was cluttered full. If Press and TV were asked to cover this, they'd want several hours a day showing nothing else: the same case, 10,000 times over, each barely identifiable, indistinguishable from the last. Unless she did something relatively original, of course, like getting herself raped or killed.

Pocock picked up the next one.

CHAPTER 6

Kenworthy entered the Copa Cabana with a stupid grin on his face, almost as if he were apologizing to the company for trespassing: not that they were all young people in here. At one table there were a couple of men, greasy-haired, and trying to be independent of social classification, who looked as if they might be resting between interviews over the Social Security counter.

The Copa Cabana had not quite made up its mind

what ambiance it wanted to evoke, for although its window display featured maracas, a poster flaunting limbo
dancers and a steel-band oil-drum, the interior seemed to
have opted for songwriter's Waikiki, with partial awnings
of straw thatch glued to the walls and photographic
murals of grass skirts and lei necklaces. All this, however,
might merely have been some throwback neurosis of the
establishment, for the excruciatingly loud music coming
from the jukebox hailed distinctly from the fringe of some
concrete jungle, the volume turned up so high that the
words were barely distinguishable. He ordered coffee,
which came to him under a froth so reminiscent of sea-
wharf scum that it was by no means certain that there was
a mouthful of viable liquid in the cup.

The lad who had sold him *The Collegian* was there,
but neither of them gave any sign that they had met. It
would have been difficult for Kenworthy to have done so,
for in going to the counter and returning to sit down with
his cup, he remained behind the boy, had no sight of him
other than the back of his head and his neck. But it was
clear that the boy had seen him, if only from the rigidity
with which he failed to make any reaction. Kenworthy
sipped at a fluid too hot for any flavour to be identified
and adjusted his body to the shock wave of sound that was
coming from the psychedelically illuminated cabinet in
the corner.

The boy was an intuitive leader and clearly, even from
this rear aspect, he was the focal point of the group with
whom he was sitting. Its other nodal figure, to judge from
the attention being paid to her by the others, was a
sallow, languorous girl in bib-and-brace denims, who was
lying back with her bottom on the front edge of her chair
and its back propping up her shoulder blades. Kenworthy
could see her full profile, and she turned once and looked
at him in slow, derisive appraisal. She appeared to have
no eyebrows and the tightness of her skin over high

cheekbones gave her a dehumanized appearance entirely at odds with her obvious vanity.

The boy had obviously whispered something to them, for there was a pointedness in the silence that came over them. They could not possibly know who he was or the reason for his being here, but from his clothes, his bearing, his expression, they would slot him into roughly the right category: roughly an enemy, and presumably an official one.

They started talking loudly now, for his benefit rather than their own. Behind the serving counter a tall, black-haired woman was standing by a sweating espresso machine, anxious not to miss anything. The girl without eyebrows made a little motion of her head in Kenworthy's direction.

'The forces are gathering, it seems.'

'I know. Does it make you feel scared?' the boy asked her. 'Would you feel safer if you changed places with me?'

'No. I don't actually feel menaced. Funny smell in here this morning, isn't there, though?'

To be provocative, Kenworthy brought *The Collegian* out of his pocket and made sure they knew what he was reading. A slight stir among them showed that they had grasped the point. The lad in the Aran sweater now partially turned his head, taking arrogant cognizance of him. Kenworthy waved the news-sheet cheerfully.

'Looks as if somebody is on to something.'

The boy shrugged his shoulders, as he had done in the tobacconist's shop. It seemed his favourite form of eloquence.

'Mind if I join you?'

Kenworthy carried his cup to their table. For a second it did not look as if anyone was prepared to make room for him. Then the boy did. The girl could have made things simpler and more comfortable by shifting her chair an inch or two, but made a point of sitting firm. One of the others said something inaudible to his neighbour.

'My name's Kenworthy. I've retired.'

The chances were that his name would mean nothing to them. Someone might conceivably have asked, retired from what? Nobody did.

'You've got a seven-day wonder on your hands, haven't you?' he said.

No one wanted to answer him. 'Shit,' sang the fashion-leader on the jukebox. It was the first recognizable word he had mouthed since Kenworthy had come in.

'I think you would be wise to bear in mind that if any of you are in possession of information that might help the police, you could be guilty of a serious offence by withholding it.'

The browless girl stood up.

'I think I'll be getting back. I want to look something up in the library before History. There is something ener-vating about the atmosphere here.'

'Sit down!' Kenworthy told her peremptorily. 'If I make you late for your next lesson, I undertake to square it for you.'

She did not want to appear to obey him, but there was something in his bark that held her back.

'Better hang on for a few minutes, Judith,' Aran Sweater said. 'This might prove interesting.'

So she dragged her chair to the opposite side of the circle, as far away from Kenworthy as she could put her-self, and sat with her face turned away from him.

'Thank you, Judith,' Kenworthy said amiably. 'And there's just one other little point I'd like to make before we get down to basics. I've taken jokes about smelly fuzz from men I had good reason to be scared of. And even then, they only bored me. If you want to be insulting, do please try to think of something new.'

No immediate answer. And then the spokesman moved things off again.

'I thought you said you were retired.'

'Quite true. Just look on me as a wandering catalyst.'

The youth looked at him with overdone comic expectancy.

'You know what a catalyst is, don't you? A substance that speeds up a chemical reaction without taking any part in it. So let's all be sensible.'

'I don't know what the fuss is all about. Two people have apparently gone off together—two people who are likely to do each other a little bit of good. Though that takes a lot of imagining—'

A snigger went round the group.

'They're both of age. I don't see where the law's being broken.'

'Then you don't know the law—which isn't always the same as what you might think common sense. If a man takes a girl away from the custody of her parents without their sanction, then the law says that's abduction.'

'The law's an ass.'

'At least, it becomes a serious offence if the intention is to have unlawful sexual relations with her. And by unlawful, the law means outside the marital bond.'

'Then the law's a blind ass.'

'As may be. But the law stands—and in the present instance, the law has it in its power to ruin lives.'

'Some lives are beyond salvage.'

'Oh? You know that, do you? Whose life in particular?'

'No one's in particular. I am speaking in general terms.'

'You are not. You are speaking in veiled specific terms—and, might I add, in a snide and despicable manner.'

The youth had either to find a smart answer or injure his image of leadership.

'We know nothing,' he said at last.

'Indeed? Yet you are printing a newspaper—even attempting to sell it to the general public—on the claim that you are about to make a revelation. There's journalism for you.'

'There's more to it than that.'

'What?'

'We've already told all we know in the local police station. And no notice has been taken of it.'

'Then repeat it for my benefit. I have no roots at all in the local station.'

'What's your interest then?'

'My interest at this stage is tentative only. I might be able to get your story listened to in the proper quarter. That's what you want, isn't it?'

In his own circle, the boy was a wit, an avant-garde philosopher, the arbiter of tone and rationale. Face to face with Kenworthy, he had to pause too long before answering.

'That's what you've said in your news-sheet, anyway, if I've got the right message out of your verbiage. But is that the way you want it? Or do you only want to make trouble? It would be a major disappointment to you to see this thing cleared up in the next few hours, wouldn't it?'

Now the others were looking at the youth expectantly, giving him perhaps his last chance.

'Perhaps one of you others—?' Kenworthy suggested, looking round their faces with an expression of puerile enthusiasm.

'Better tell him, Justin,' Judith said with languid disgust. 'And then we can all get back to the Treaty of Utrecht.'

Justin shifted in his chair with a fidget of relief.

'It's just that on Tuesday morning Everard and Sue were both on the eight-five. But they were careful not to see each other on the platform, and they didn't travel in the same part of the train.'

'Just one little moment. You seem pretty well informed—'

'There are a lot of commuters on that train. Pete's father, for one—'

A boy at the other side of the table raised his eyes in acknowledgement.

'And Dave's mother was taking his sister on a pre-Register Office shopping orgy.'

'Go on.'

'Sue had an interview at St Bart's Training College. Everard was absent without leave.'

'Reneging on his responsibility for our moral welfare,' Judith said.

'Leaving us to our own devices. We can't imagine how he could bear to think of what might be going on behind his back during third period on a Tuesday morning.'

Justin had rapidly regained confidence, and another round of sniggering helped him.

'Go on,' Kenworthy said.

'Well, they met just outside the ticket barrier at Marylebone, each knowing damned well that the other had been on the train. Dave's mother saw that. There was not an inkling of surprise about either of them. And then he took her off to the station buffet, of all places.'

Laughter, quite out of proportion to the quality of the joke, cementing the group, giving some clue to the degree of nervous tension.

'And that was the last Dave's mother saw of them— going into the buffet? I must say I haven't heard anything sinister yet.'

'Dave's mother came home on the five twenty-eight. And she saw the pair of them arrive separately in the forecourt—and then go off together.'

'Back to the buffet?'

Kenworthy was not above tagging along with what passed off as their sense of humour.

'No. Out of the station altogether.'

'And?'

'Well—that's it. They went off somewhere in London together.'

'And the local police were not too interested in all this?'

'Merely sneered.'

'Maybe they thought it would be a waste of time putting out a national call for every potential witness who'd been outside a London terminus at afternoon peak hour a week ago.'

'It does happen to be the last time that anyone who knew them set eyes on them.'

'So what do you think ought to happen now?'

'A serious effort to find them.'

'Why?'

Justin slewed in his chair and looked at him with pathetic surprise.

'Look—whose side are you on? Don't *you* think they ought to be found?'

'Naturally. But I'm surprised that you do. Ten minutes ago you were blithely talking about two people doing each other some good, if I remember correctly.'

'You don't know the personalities concerned,' Justin said.

'Fill me in, then.'

'Everard's such a bloody hypocrite, that's what it's all about.'

'For example?'

'He wants to take us back to the Dark Ages. Do you know, he even quoted *Piers Plowman* at Judith, telling her to save her pure body for her only love?'

'I dare say that sounded a little less priggish in its proper context.'

'It's not easy to do justice to him. The man's so mealy-mouthed it just isn't true.'

'You don't care for diversity of opinion in your Utopia?'

'It isn't that. It isn't that at all. It's that the man's so morally impregnable—or so he'd have us think—and then he has to go off on a dirty detour with Sue Shires of all people.'

'You seem pretty sure of that fact.'

'It stands out a mile.'

'All right. For the sake of the present argument, I'll accept that for the time being. Now tell me where Sue Shires fits into your social picture.'

'Another one too good to be true: an honest ploughman's wench in the true Everard mould. But don't get me wrong. Eduardo didn't have the moulding of her. She came to us ready-made: by Bell, Book and Candle out of Hearth and Home.'

'What do you mean by that—if anything?'

'She's a good little girl: a communicant Anglican who couldn't bear to miss the chalice, and she has parents whom she wants to be proud of her. She is a disgustingly strenuous worker with a second-class brain—and is victim of the fate that befalls so many second-class brains. She is going to be a teacher.'

'Would you say that Everard had a second-class brain?' Kenworthy asked, with a hint of genuine interest in the answer.

'A moot point. Opinion is divided. As a linguist he commands respect: though as far as he is concerned, neither the French nor the German language has undergone any organic development since the 1940s.'

'You mean he is not as up to date as you are in contemporary slang?'

'A neat point,' Justin said, with a suggestion of magnanimity. 'But I could argue that a man in his position, teaching scholarship classes, ought to be on top of current gutter-talk too. That's beside the point. I think he might once have had the makings of a first-class intellect. But he's so hemmed in—partly by major mistakes that he's made in his life—'

'Do you mind if I tell you you're an arrogant young

sod?' Kenworthy said, and there was a touch of galvanized silence. Justin broke it with a short and artificial laugh and his shoulders twitched in their involuntary tic.

'Have it your own way.'

'It's been hinted that Susan Shires had an adolescent crush on your Mr Everard. Have you anything to tell me about that?'

'We used to pull her leg on that score, but I for one never thought there was anything in it. You see, we gave Eduardo a bad time sometimes, I've got to admit that. He was fair game, especially if ever a moral issue came up. Very easily shocked — and we certainly used to shock him.'

He laughed, this time genuinely, at a real memory.

'Do you remember that time Judith as good as asked him how many times a week he had it? The poor devil actually blushed. And anybody could tell he was a Monday, Thursday and Saturday man.'

'How?' Kenworthy asked, staccato.

'I would have thought that was obvious. Saturday night for a long lie-in after a major exertion. Monday because he has us for two bloody hours and has to have something to look forward to to get through the day. Thursday to keep his seminal vesicles working to an efficient balance.'

'May we get back to Susan Shires?' Kenworthy asked.

'She used to leap to his defence when we were being specially hard on him. In her best Sunday School manner, you understand. She was always one to fight shy of the proper names for things. So we started telling her she was only jealous of Blanche.'

'Blanche?'

'Mrs Everard.'

'But there was never anything concrete between them?'

'Nothing whatever. Entirely the product of our satirical imagination.'

'No extra tuition out of school hours?'

Justin grinned.

'No. We leave that to the music department.'

'No volunteering to help him in his stockroom at the end of term?'

'I see you know how it's done. No—nothing like that.'

'Had the Shires girl ever been abroad with one of Everard's organized parties?'

'She went last Easter to Caudebec.'

'Did that give rise to any rumours?'

'Difficult to tell what was rumour and what was mere teasing. There wouldn't be much on in Caudebec. Sir would be otherwise occupied.'

Kenworthy fixed him with a sobering eye.

'Is there any truth in these Caudebec tales?'

'I wouldn't think so. From all accounts, Marie-Thérèse was a safe companion for him. You are well informed, aren't you?'

'It's become a habit with me, over the years. And there's one thing that strikes me very forcibly indeed.'

Justin looked at him with sincere curiosity: the two acknowledged leaders in the room publicly admitting their interest in each other.

'What's that?'

'That anything between John Everard and Sue Shires is extremely improbable,' Kenworthy said.

'I disagree.'

Justin's tone and facial seriousness gave the impression that he thought himself a move ahead of his opponent's game.

'Our teasing of Sue has been—shall we say, unremitting? It may have had the effect of subliminal advertising.'

'I think you are completely unprincipled,' Kenworthy said.

'Of course. Why should I carry a sack of wet sand about on my shoulders? That, by the way, is a misquote from Emerson. But why do you say so in this particular respect?'

'Because you are running a campaign that's going to ruin the couple.'

'Sue will come to no ultimate harm.'

'And Everard?'

'I said at the outset: he's a hypocrite. That's the offence we never forgive.'

A grunt of approval from his disciples.

'Rubbish!' Kenworthy said. 'You're all so damned bored you can't think of a better way of amusing yourselves.'

'Besides which, it's time for college's sake that the language side got into the hands of someone in touch with the contemporary world.'

'That's surely a matter for your headmaster.'

'The Shepherd's all right. But he's an administrator, no sort of scholar. He got his doctorate in educational statistics. Academically, he doesn't know what's happening around him.'

'I'm beginning to see what is meant by pupil power.'

'Devastating, isn't it?'

'What time do you have to be back in school?'

Justin looked at the crystal display of his digital watch.

'Tutorial in Modern History began twenty minutes ago.'

'I'll come along with you, if I may. You can show me where your headmaster's study is.'

Alfred Shepherd, Ph.D., M.Ed., D.P.A., was a small man with a large bald head, a very new casual suit, with a light but pronounced check pattern — and, apparently, a total readiness to have a large amount of his time taken up without notice. He was a busy man. His secretary's office was a showground for contemporary word-processing equipment and there were more wall charts and mobile indices in his study than there were books. It was, however, only the working nature of these exhibits that pointed to his vocation. He might otherwise have been taken for some trade representative of some product capable of selling itself. He did not know Kenworthy, had clearly never heard of him, yet seemed unaffected by Kenworthy's initial insistence that he was without standing in the matter he had come to discuss. But first there was the apology for having kept students out of their tutorial. Dr Shepherd did not seem to mind in the least.

'You've probably done them the world of good—let them see things through somebody else's eyes.'

'I certainly don't see life through theirs.'

'No. It's all a kaleidoscope of phases and fashions,' the headmaster said.

'There's this story going about that one of your staff has gone off with one of the girls. Your pupils seem to believe it.'

'Well, they'd be the ones to know, of course.'

'Doesn't it trouble you?'

'Trouble me?'

'The reputation of your school—to consider it on only one level.'

'If I worried about the reputation of the school, in that sense—we prefer to call it a college, by the way—if tittle-tattle worried me, I'd be living on barbiturates by now—like our senior mistress.'

'Why? Does this sort of thing often happen?'

'What, elopement of pupils and staff? No; I think it's the first time we've actually had this situation.'

'Does it surprise you?'

'Human behaviour is by definition the sum total of what humans do. It never surprises me, Superintendent.'

'Ex-Superintendent.'

'Ex-Superintendent.'

'Mrs Everard is hoping to retain me to look for her husband.'

'Jolly good. The sooner you find him the better. I can't

claim it isn't a headache, having a key man away.'

'This incident, this episode—won't it affect Everard's tenure of office?'

'I expect some of the Governors will tend to make heavy weather of it. They'll enjoy having their self-righteous say. It will run on for months, of course, if they want to dismiss him.'

'What can you tell me about him?'

'Everard? An elitist, by temperament, training and experience, which won't do, of course. It comes, I think, from his having been cock of some pretty trivial little academic dunghill when he was a boy. He never got over it, so I can hardly expect him to get over it now. Oh no—I'm stuck with Everard, but I might have been stuck with worse. He works hard. More's the pity, I often think.'

'There must have been serious tension between him and some of his classes.'

'Some years worse than others. It's a question of personalities.'

'Which this year are clashing badly, I think?'

'I have been aware of some backlash. There has been a case referred from college council to college cabinet, but we could do no more than allow it to remain on the table. The only man who can alter things is Everard himself and he won't, hasn't got it in him, so I don't propose to lose any sleep over it.'

Kenworthy gave up trying to make head or tail of an abstract hanging on the headmaster's wall and looked the man in the eye.

'Is it a boy called Justin who's the biggest thorn in his side?'

'Justin Fairbrother. His name's not Justin at all, really. He made that amendment himself when he moved from the second-tier comprehensive. A clever boy. A very clever boy indeed.'

'Not sometimes irresponsible?'

'I wouldn't say so. On the look-out for an identity, which I suppose applies to most of us most of the time. He makes a mistake now and then—better for him to make them here than out in the world.'

'No matter what they cost Everard?'

'If Everard can't stand up to an eighteen-year-old, there isn't much I can do about it. Any protection I gave him would merely be artificial, would merely postpone the evil day.'

'Aren't you at all worried by this news-sheet that the Fairbrother boy is involved with.'

'I try not to be. Sooner or later they're going to run into serious trouble, and sometimes I think the sooner the better. But then, you see, I'm only human myself—and uncharitable enough to like easy ways served out to me on a plate.'

'Susan Shires?'

The headmaster pulled an enigmatic face; it might have been a declaration of uncertainty—or he might even have harboured a strong dislike for the girl.

'A mouse. Not top drawer, either intellectually or emotionally. Primary teaching is about her ceiling.'

'Is it feasible that she has become infatuated with Everard?'

'These things happen.'

'And what is your policy when it does?'

'How can I have a policy about a thing like that? The only people who can control it are the principals in the action. If people need outside help, then it is usually no use to them because they are beyond it. I should go off my head in a place like this if I tried to run my life on any other lines. This is a busy·college, ex-Superintendent. I have to save my energy for what is positive.'

'Would it be very unprofessional of me to ask your opinion of Mrs Everard?'

'Highly unprofessional—but not so unprofessional as

any answer I could give you. Yes: I can sum her up for you, I think. Uninvolved. And that, of course, is the besetting sin here. People have got to be involved. They've got to identify. Otherwise there's no way of making a place like this work.'

'But she isn't a member of your staff, Headmaster.'

'Nevertheless.'

Bells rang about the building and someone knocked on the headmaster's door. He took no notice.

'Nevertheless, if she won't involve herself, won't identify, she's a chink in my armour. I won't say she's the only one, by a long chalk. I can't do anything about it, of course.'

'I mustn't take up any more of your time. You're obviously up to the eyes in it. But one more question: has Everard a friend on the staff? I mean, someone in whom you'd expect him to confide: someone perhaps who came over with him from the old school?'

The friendliest of smiles spread over the headmaster's lips.

'*The old school.* How readily that phrase trips off your lips. Quite like a well-oiled machine. I do believe you're an elitist yourself, ex-Superintendent.'

'Unashamedly,' Kenworthy said.

'If I were you, I'd try Sam Swarbrick, my senior historian. You'll find him a very different sort of character from Everard. He has adapted.'

'Can you give me his home address?'

'My secretary can—and shouldn't—but undoubtedly will.'

CHAPTER 7

A man and a girl went into a pub on the Highgate side of Hampstead Heath and the landlord, who was a former army warrant officer, queried the girl's age when she asked for a gin and tonic.

'You ought to know better,' he said officiously to the man, who must have been over the fifty mark, and could have been a civil servant or city clerk. What was odd was the man's reaction. For instead of losing his temper, or preposterously trying to claim that it was the girl's birthday today, he shushed her out of the bar as smartly as if they had just succeeded in rifling the till. The landlord, who liked to identify himself publicly with the keeping of a good house, immediately rang the police. He did not have to look up the number of the local station.

But the squad car was unable to find the couple.

A man with a lot of hair and a very large moustache, as well as a velvet head-band reminiscent of an Indian brave, was picked up by a pair of uniformed women in the Haymarket in company with a girl who could have been as young as fourteen and had put on make-up as if she were not in total control of her hands. When asked, by way of a test question, who she was, he replied that he did not know, that he had only within the last half-hour won her on a pinball machine. Being suspected of frivolity, he was asked to accompany the officers to their headquarters, where he persisted in his story despite a heartfelt backhander across the mouth from the Station Sergeant.

Separated from her escort, the girl, who was only twelve years old and educationally subnormal, was traced to her home by a very simple conversational trick.

The man, who was a poet, though with his public ac-
claim still to earn, repeated his story that he had been in
the Crystal Rooms in the Strand when he had seen her
leaning over one of the machines with a man who was ex-
pressing voluble displeasure at her company. Believing
that she would be better off with him, the poet had
offered to provide coins for the slot provided that she was
put up as stakes. There had been a danger of a fight
before his good faith was recognized, but his offer had
eventually been taken up, and he had won her with a
score of 17,500.

A shred of cannabis resin, source of previous lyrical in-
spiration, was found among the fluff in his pocket, and he
was duly passed into channels with which he was already
familiar.

Mrs Gladys Turnbull needed to cross the landing only a
few minutes after she had seen her lodgers cross the road
back to the Coastguard from the sand dunes. She paused
by the door of Room 3 and had the satisfaction of hearing
the rhythmic creak of the bed, punctuated by an occasional whimper.

The next morning, the couple were uncommunicative
with each other at breakfast-time, the man largely absorbed in his newspaper. They did not linger after the
meal, having already carried their cases to the car before
they ate. The woman who came daily to do the bedrooms
called the landlady as soon as she saw the state of the bed.

'The poor wee innocent,' Mrs Turnbull said. 'I wonder
if it really was them?'

Looking round for any evidence that might justify
future name-dropping, she found a small crumpled
envelope in the wastepaper basket and unscrewed it. It
was of the kind in which public servants are often given
their pay slips, and the name John Everard had been written on it in blue ballpoint.

She glued it into a scrapbook in which she kept mementoes of such encounters as she had had—usually more remote and oblique than this one—with anyone whose name was in the news.

In Hertfordshire, Inspector Pocock put on one side a memorandum from a woman officer, suggesting that a girl picked up in a pub raid the previous evening might possibly be the escapee from a mental hospital who had thus sought liberty for the fourth time.

The girl had had to be kept in cells overnight, since the only available reception centre was full. Even after that suggestive hardship, she was still obstinate about not revealing her identity. The inspector sent one of his crime cars to pick up the social worker who had handled Penny Bentham last time.

But the girl in the cells was not Penny Bentham.

'I'm sorry Penny's bust out again,' the social worker said. 'She was said to be making progress. We were supposed to be starting arrangements to see how she'd shape up to a spell outside. Still, I suppose that proves that she wasn't ready for it. This has happened before, you know. One nurse goes on leave—the only one in the whole institution who understands her, Penny says—and three days later she is sleeping under the stars again. What are you going to do with the lass downstairs?'

'She'll belong to you, sooner or later.'

CHAPTER 8

Sam Swarbrick was, as his headmaster had suggested, a very different personality from John Everard.

He was in no way put out to receive an evening visit from Kenworthy—gave the impression, in fact, that he rather thought he was going to enjoy it: another man of the age that so many of them were—Kenworthy, and Kenworthy's wife, and Everard, and Blanche Everard, and Marie-Thérèse Besson, and the woman in Schleswig-Holstein. He was wearing bedroom slippers and a very loose cardigan, and was reading a paperback Colin Watson. His furniture was old, his books had overflowed to the sideboard, and his wife was ironing in the same room so as not to miss television.

'Ah, yes—you're the man who made half my class late for the Treaty of Utrecht.'

'This is a liberty on my part. You're perfectly entitled to throw me into the street. Only if you're going to, will you do it now, please, so that I don't have to waste the entire evening?'

Kenworthy, robbed of status if not of authority, was perhaps a little too sensitive about his amateur presence.

'Far from it, dear man. I know what you're here for, and if I can help, I will.'

He neither looked nor sounded the type of man with whom Justin and Judith would expect to make much headway. From behind him, Kenworthy heard the creak and pressure of Dorothy Swarbrick's iron.

'Give me a few off-the-cuff answers to a salvo of questions, then. For a start, has John Everard gone off with Sue Shires?'

'I wouldn't think so. Not unless he's taken her somewhere to read a set book with her.'

'Seriously?'

'No.'

'Secondly, then: has he gone to northern Germany to his immediate post-war mistress?'

'Never having met the lady, I wouldn't think it safe to speculate. I know about her, of course. He's talked about her quite frankly. She looked after his spiritual and intellectual interests at a time when there wasn't much spirit or intellect about. And it didn't stop at that. Not by any means. But I know him pretty well. We've been colleagues for over twelve years; fought many a battle together: staff meetings at the old place, committees, councils, cabinets and quangos at the new. And he certainly didn't hanker after her.'

'And Marie-Thérèse Besson?'

'Caudebec en Caux? Madame Bovary's home town? Do you know, we used to call her Emma, when we were pulling his leg. But, no. A nice woman. I met her once or twice when I was out with him on one of his jaunts. But barely beddable. In any case, I doubt if she was interested, and I'm damned sure Jack wasn't. We used to rib him mercilessly about her, and I'm sorry we did, because somebody was indiscreet and it tracked over to the kids. There was a three-times-removed hint about it in the school magazine, and Jack was terribly upset.'

A creak of the iron. 'I think it's shameful, the way that man's been treated,' Dorothy Swarbrick said. 'It's a wonder he hasn't had a breakdown years ago.'

'He does rather ask for it, darling.'

'And of course,' Kenworthy said, 'he's up against some artful operators in this year's sixth.'

'They're all bloody sixth—you haven't got the hang of us yet, Kenworthy. You ought to see some of the material that's being further educated. I have to start each year with a literacy course. But, that apart, Justin Fairbrother's a bastard. He's bad, that young man: regards anybody's integrity as a personal challenge. He doesn't try it on with me—partly, I think, because he suspects that I could be as nasty as he is, if I chose. But Jack Everard was God's gift to him. And they're unkind to Sue Shires—that's something that may or may not have a bearing on the case. But either Fairbrother or Everard has had to win; and it looks as if Jack's lost.'

'Shame!' came from the ironing-board.

'You really think that it is Fairbrother who finally pushed him overboard?'

'Didn't you get a close enough look to come to the same conclusion yourself?'

'Not to be sure. But I'm prepared to take your word for it.'

'Jack was a sick man, anyway. But you can't use that as a defence against kids. Even he knew that. And I did my best to help him, in my tiny way—but you can't make a man's personal relationships for him. His outlook was sweetly simplistic: he knew more than his students, had greater experience, more knowledge of life and men, therefore he was an authoritarian, a writer of the tablets, not just a bringer of them down from the mountain.'

'Sounds rather like being a Superintendent instead of a sergeant. What's the opposition view?'

'Oh, it's a free for all, we're all in it on equal terms, the search after knowledge, the determination of a working regime, the devising of a code of discipline.'

'That's your headmaster's point of view?'

Kenworthy heard the iron laid to rest.

'I'll go and make coffee,' Mrs Swarbrick said. 'And you can get the bad language over before I get back.'

But actually, Swarbrick did not fly off any handles.

'The headmaster,' he said, 'doesn't believe in anything—which he kids himself is believing in everything. The place has two dozen committees—and one unofficial one, that meets in one corner of the staff room at coffee time—a handful of old-timers who quietly see that the place works. The place does work—but it isn't the survival of the fittest; there's too great an element of luck about it. If a dispute does arise, as it has to at times, then the old man opts for the solution that brings him the quietest life. That means that pupils win—and staff who stick their neck out lose. Jack sticks his neck out: even about the size of his pupils' weekly work assignments. You lose face when you have to climb down. Me—I never let anyone see me climbing up.'

Dorothy Swarbrick brought in the coffee and joined them round the fire for ten minutes.

'What—no blood vessels burst?'

'Mr Kenworthy knows what it's all about. There's no need for pyrotechnics.'

'Have you told him about Justin—his family circumstances?'

Swarbrick charged his pipe, and Kenworthy did the same.

'No; there's a point. What do you think, Kenworthy? How do you picture him? What sort of background?'

'Oh, I don't know. Father probably at least a head of hair higher than the average man hereabouts. Entrepreneurial type perhaps—though on not too exalted a level. Could be a dog-track bookmaker. Money no problem. It was probably touch and go at one time whether the boy went to minor public school or your comprehensive. Then the old man came down on the side of the locals, decided the lad ought to learn what makes run-of-the-mill mortals tick.'

'Remarkable, Holmes. And you dug all that out of one meeting with the boy?'

'I must say you've got me talking more loosely than I usually do.'

'Yes, well, we'll excuse you this time. I see your point of view. Justin is suave, witty, rock-firm confident in public, has a one-off IQ. All set for an Open Award next December—if the dons don't take fright at the sight of him. Actually, his father is a retired wages-clerk from the dry-battery factory. Mother and father are elderly, and they had him late, only son. I met them at our last at-home, when parents come to see how their offspring are doing. And I have never seen a couple looking more lost in my life. We just don't know what's going on behind the scenes with half these kids. If young Justin's a bastard at school, that's nothing to the life that he leads them at home. There's no rapport, no rapport whatsoever between him and them. He has contempt for their ignorance, their simplicity, their decency. They try to understand what modern schoolwork is about — and they can't. His mother hates to hear the door open when he comes home from afternoon school. He berates them for the books that they read, the newspaper they take, the shows that they watch on TV. The Duke, they call him, because he expects them to wait on him hand and foot.'

Swarbrick was having trouble with a stopped-up stem. He reached for a pipe cleaner from the mantelpiece.

'And here's a strange thing about him — one that I've never heard anyone comment on, and I doubt if he's truly aware of it himself: he's a boy who can do anything with his fingers — absolutely effortless control. He even takes notes in a perfect Chancery hand, truly elegant — and at top speed.'

'What's his future?'

'The law, he says. He wants the bar.'

'That's the one walk in life where a youngster still needs grubstaking.'

'It's going to be very interesting to watch.'

Swarbrick tried again, put away his rogue pipe and tested two others. Presently he was producing blue smoke.

'You said just now,' Kenworthy said, 'that Master Fairbrother has a thing against other people's integrity.'

'I don't think that's too uncommon, is it? The sport of kings — and of dole queues.'

'Yes — a game for one or more players. Clubs, societies — whole nations can play at it. But in the hands of a skilled operator, it can have fatal consequences.'

'I would say that young Fairbrother is just about at the prime of his excellence.'

'And how about Susan Shires's integrity?'

Swarbrick gave it some thought, crossing one dis-reputable slipper over the instep of the other.

'I wouldn't expect it to interest him—except at some moment of quite abysmal boredom.'

'Or perhaps to alleviate the boredom of lesser-minded followers?'

'That's a possibility. But I'm not sure that integrity is the right word to use of our Sue. Naïvety, rather. No: I'm not being that kind of snob. Jack Everard's integrity is a personal ethic. Susan's is a code she's latched on to. I see a lot of youngsters go through it: churchy, evangelistic, dogmatic and dutiful. Not many of them carry it into their twenties, though I think Susan might. But I don't think it would tempt Justin. From his point of view, Sue isn't big enough to be worth breaking.'

'Except perhaps as a possible weapon for the destruction of Everard?'

Swarbrick considered it slowly, and with obvious anxiety.

'I hope you're wrong about that,' he said eventually.

'Much crime in your college?' Kenworthy asked, with a breezy change of tone.

'Some. It comes in waves. We've had shoplifting on an organized basis. Complete with channels for disposing of the loot. That's been cleared up, though. And it goes without saying that Fairbrother and Co. are not in that league.'

'Alcohol?'

'That's difficult, with the permitted age running plumb down the middle of us. The police have brought one or two cases of under-age drinking in pubs; and there are private parties which, the old man rightly says, are none of our business.'

'Drugs?'

'There are always some about. I've smelled a reefer on the touchline at a first eleven match. Amphetamines seem easiest to get; as playthings, really, that's the trouble. The police have suspected pushers in the town, and they once planted plain-clothes women at an end-of-term dance. But they dug nothing up.'

'How about the Fairbrother set?'

'They'll have experimented. They *must* have experimented. But nobody's hooked, and I'm pretty sure there's nothing going on at the moment.'

'We live in stirring times, don't we? Sex?'

'Ugly and hydra-headed as ever. So far, we've had three married couples doing A-levels. And there was a complication a year ago when a young economics graduate, newcomer to the staff, wanted to wed one of our own girls in the middle of his second term. The head, of course, stayed out of it, but the common room was split down the middle. The matter resolved itself, because the parents took the girl away, and a week or two later, we heard the whole thing was off.'

'I presume there's some promiscuity?'

'Now what can possibly have put that idea into your head? Comparatively rare, as far as one can get to know. They generally pair themselves off, with a remarkable loyalty rate, which lasts the necessary one or two years until higher education sorts them out afresh. There are ardent discussions among some of the male staff as to which girl is and which isn't on the Pill. I'd say about half of them are; I hope so, anyway. It's the normally good girls who have the accidents.'

'Like Susan Shires?'

'I wish you wouldn't keep putting these horrid thoughts into my head.'

'And how about Justin and Judith?'

'Judith is way, way, way out of Justin's class. She can't touch his brains, his resolution, probably only half understands his aspirations. But she has staying-power. She's Queen-Bee because she's Justin's girl, and that's how it's been since the first week they came here.'

'How, when and where do they get together?'

'I don't know.'

'What's Judith's attitude to Susan?'

'As far as I can see, Susan behaves the same way to everybody, but I'd say that Judith hardly notices her.'

'How much we know—and how little,' Kenworthy said.

'Yet try to wind ourselves too high, for sinful man beneath the sky. That's what Jack Everard could never learn not to do.'

'I must go. My last chance of getting home tonight.'

'Well, do come back, as often as you like. I'm dying to know—'

'I may. All things are possible.'

Kenworthy had phoned Elspeth that he would be home between midnight and one. He had wondered what frame of mind she would be in. There was every possibility that this would be too realistic a reminder of the old days, the sudden calls, the family commitments that had had to be shunted, with weak apologies, into second place.

She was waiting up for him—and had his slippers ready. She did not seem to be hankering for bed and listened with an almost schoolgirlish sense of romance to the story that he had to tell. At the same time, she interpolated an occasional alert and incisive question.

'And I suppose the main question now is who's going to pay for a round trip to North Germany, Normandy and the Tirolean Alps?'

'I really hadn't given that more than a scanty thought.'

'I can see it formulated in your mind. I doubt whether Mrs Everard could do more than finance a very basic tour.'

'I doubt whether she can. And it would be money ill spent—especially if it restores the status quo.'

'It's just the same as it always was, isn't it? You did all that you thought was right, but the real arbiter as to whether it ever did anybody any good was the imbecility or otherwise of the law. You can only do what people want you to; you can't make up their minds for them.'

'You honestly think I ought to try? Or is it just your curiosity getting the better of you?'

'What I'm trying to say, Simon, is that you've been needing this. And if you want to use some of your own savings to go swanning about the continent in reasonable comfort, there'll be no come-back from me. Get what you can off expenses, of course, but you promised yourself a retirement holiday, and then never had one. And you know what you're like on a holiday: it's useless having nothing to do.'

'It would probably be a waste of time, from several points of view. You've heard the yarn: where do *you* think he is?'

'I hope he's at some stage or other of his pilgrimage to Italy, that he'll get to the top of his footpath—and come down again with things clearer in his mind.'

'You know what you are, don't you?'

And she looked at him with her eyebrows comically arched in query.

'An incurable romantic,' he said, 'though fortunately not only in the literary and aesthetic sense.'

'On the contrary, I am a realist.'

'How do you figure that out?'

'I know what you'd be like to live with if you were on the staff of that school: rather like your last few years at the Yard.'

'I'll give it one more twizzle. I'll go back in the morning and make myself known in the Warnford nick, see if they've anything frying. They won't be delighted to see me. I don't know anyone there, and someone is going to say, *Who?*'

'They might even have broken the case by now—or be well on the way.'

'I wonder. They're obviously not saying in public whether they believe it's an elopement or not. Ten thousand missing persons a year, and an adult is entitled to do what he pleases with his freedom, as long as he stays inside the law. That will have been the response over the desk. But if the inspector is worth his salt, he'll be taking a quiet look round on his own account, just to be one ahead if the wind does start to blow. I'll hold a wet finger up, anyway. And then I'll pop round to see Blanche Everard again and tell her whether I'm on or not.'

'You'll be on, Simon.'

CHAPTER 9

Hunstanton: an Edwardian setting whose later accretions seemed somehow pushed back into their proper, unobtrusive place by the out-of-season bluster of the elements on the cliff top. One could stand on the Green, with its fringe of sandstone hotels, and recapture something of what the pre-First World War crowd had seen; though the railway station had gone, and the pierhead was changed, and the shopping-streets leaned towards super-marketing.

The couple walked on the deserted cliff top with the salt wind on their faces. Then the man—sometime Joseph Kite, sometime William Townshend, and *known* to Gladys Turnbull to be John Everard (and now, incidentally, signing the Visitors' Book as Kenneth Burgess) conducted the girl back to one of the Edwardian hotels and then returned to the town centre, where he indulged in some specialized shopping. This included some clothes for the girl: he kept telling her he wanted her to be more feminine.

He also went to a chemist's, where his request at first

seemed to puzzle and then worry the white-coated assistant. She disappeared into the dispensary and came back
with the pharmacist himself, who did all he could to show
that he was taking his customer very seriously indeed. At
the end of a patient discussion, however, he shook his
head negatively, whereupon the man produced something from his wallet with which, it appeared to two
women who were studying a cosmetic display, he tried
hard to explain or perhaps justify his request. He came
away empty-handed.

His next call was at a stationer's, where he was disap-
pointed that the evening papers had not yet arrived. He
bought a copy of each of the morning editions that were
still in stock and retired with them to one of the cliff
shelters, where he went rapidly through one after the
other of them, in spite of squally draughts that made
them awkward to handle.

Then he went to the reading room annexed to the
county library and went through three of the morning
editions that he had not already seen, showing unmasked
irritability because the *Eastern Daily Press* was for a long
time monopolized by an elderly man with a chipped mag-
nifying glass. On his return to the hotel, he still seemed
obsessed by the press, and went rummaging in the residents' lounge for anything he could find, even asking two
old maids for the copy of the *East Anglian Times* that was
wedged under one of their cushions. Nothing that he
found to read seemed to bring him any joy.

That evening he again dined alone, but did not ask for
anything to be sent up to his roommate. Nor did he go up
to visit her after the meal, but buttoned his overcoat
about his neck and went into a public bar in the centre of
the town, where he drank three pints of beer.

It was here that he was joined by a man younger than
himself—a man who had gone through a routine of
grooming himself, though neither his natural features nor

his frayed suit gave much basis for a fastidious appearance. Nevertheless, his hair was oiled and his shabby tie had once, it looked probable, been the token of some club, school or regiment; doubtless a relatively obscure one, in whatever case. He was also wearing sunglasses, despite the yellow-walled gloom of the bar. After a minute or two of apparently reflective silence, he opened a conversation—and persisted in it despite lack of encouragement.

'Not as bad as it might be for the time of the year.'

'No.'

'I mean, we're getting on with it, aren't we? Every week's a week less. It makes it a long winter when the rough stuff starts before Christmas.'

'M'm.'

'When you think of what last year was like, we were well into it by this time.'

To this the older man did not reply at all, but took temporary refuge in his mug.

'Yes—it makes spring seem a long way off when the snow starts in November.'

'M'm.'

'Your name's Everard, isn't it?'

And at this the man was startled. He got out a packet of cigarettes, and his right hand was trembling as he lit one.

'Oh, don't worry, mate. I'm not going to shop you. Whatever you're up to, that's your business. I saw you carrying your bags into the Braemar, and I thought to myself, that'll be them. Nice-looking piece. I should think she's a reasonable rattle, isn't she?'

'Look—I don't know you. I don't know what you're talking about.'

'Come off it! You're in all the papers. And you can't say you weren't buying them up this afternoon, because I saw you. Still, I think you stand a reasonable chance. The photographs aren't up to much: could be anybody. The one of you's pretty old. You've changed enough to get away with it since you last played tennis. And the one of the girl's much too young; girls change completely. And as I say, I'm not going to say a dicky-bird.'

Somebody put money in the jukebox and a Country and Western guitar made hard work of conversation.

'I should think it would be worth twenty quid to you,' the younger man said.

'I beg your pardon?'

'I was thinking: twenty quid seems a fair price.'

'You must be off your head.'

'I don't think so. Not the way I see it. I mean, they're going to chuck a deskful of books at you, when they do put a hand on your shoulder. Her parents are up in arms about it. Your wife was on telly tonight, pleading with you to come back and settle things. It'll mean what they call a High Court injunction.'

'None of this has anything to do with me.'

'No? You weren't at the Coastguard last night, either, I suppose?'

Gladys Turnbull had been unable to resist the temptation to show her precious envelope to one of the more trusted of her fishermen guests. Her exhortations to confidence had been worth no more than the breath on which they were spoken.

'Interlude on the beach in the moonlight, too, I believe.'

'Look, for God's sake keep your bloody voice down.'

'Twenty quid.'

'I haven't got twenty quid on me.'

'That's all right. There are ways and means. I can wait till the banks open.'

'Take a fiver.'

'Don't be so bloody mean, mate. I'm up against inflation, same as you are.'

'A fiver now and another in the morning.'

'How much have you got on you?'

And here the older man showed himself naïvely incautious—perhaps the result of a life sheltered from the likes of the man to whom he was talking. He brought out his wallet to look, and seeing two five-pound notes and two singles, the blackmailer helped himself to the fives with a deft thumb and forefinger.

'That leaves you as much as you'll want for drink tonight—and you can buy me a Scotch, while you're about it. I'll be about by the time you've had your breakfast.

But the couple breakfasted in peace, not even finding much to say to each other. When they emerged into the chill of the car park, the man was standing just outside the drive-in, looking up at a wheeling seagull.

It was swift and neat, the way he gave them the slip. The man known in the Braemar as Kenneth Burgess put their bags down behind the boot of a green Volvo in the furthest corner from where his own car stood parked. The blackmailer chose the shortest distance between two points and started to come up alongside the wall of the hotel, whereupon his quarry snatched the bags and with unexpected agility dashed diagonally to his red Escort. The girl was not with him; she was waiting by the front entrance to the Braemar. The man leaned over to the catch of the passenger door. The car did not actually come to a standstill. They were away.

For the first time since anyone had observed this pair, the girl was actually grinning. She looked over her shoulder at the angry figure in the car park and he could almost hear her laughing.

The couple did not continue their circuit of the coast. They went back the way they had come, following the seaboard road towards Brancaster and Wells.

A police constable, called by the excitable owner of a

small Trattoria off Greencoat Place, SW1, found a
Spanish girl sobbing over a cup of coffee for which she
had only been able to offer pesetas in payment. She found
police station tea particularly distasteful, and it was some
time before an interpreter could be found (a still room
hand from a hotel in the Wilton Road) who helped to get
from her a coherent story of how she had taken impulsive
flight from the stranger who had come to meet her at Victoria Station. He was duly telephoned to come and fetch
her.

The couple in the red hire-car drove away from Hunstanton and stopped for petrol in Blakeney. Late in the morning they pulled up at the head of a steep, narrow lane
distinguished by a crooked fingerpost that said *Beach*.
They walked down this lane together, holding hands and
swinging arms.

At lunch-time the man ate a bar snack at a substantial
hotel in the village of Weybourne.

He was alone.

CHAPTER 10

As he had forecast to Elspeth, Kenworthy was not the
most welcome caller at Warnford police station at eleven
o'clock the next morning. But he seemed to be expected,
though his name, four months after his retirement, did
not seem to excite the clerks in the outer office. But he
was taken straight to the office of the inspector who was
handling the case: a man called Leyton, aged about
thirty-five, with close-cut gollywog hair, Kentish vowels
and an unimpressively laborious low-key attitude to the
whole affair. But he knew that Kenworthy had called on
Blanche Everard, he knew that he had seen the head-

master and Sam Swarbrick, so he was obviously deeper into the case than he wanted it to appear.

'So you're working on behalf of Mrs Everard?'

'I don't know yet. I haven't made up my mind.'

'It's your decision, of course. It's not for me to try to influence you. But frankly, I think you'd be wasting your time. The man's had some sort of breakdown, that's certain. He's physically sick, too, and his greatest danger's a heart attack, at the first real onset of which we hope he will get himself hospitalized. That's the view of his GP, and of the consultant who sees him periodically at the hospital. It's to be hoped that he won't be too far from telephones and ambulances if symptoms do occur. We hope, in fact, that he'll not leave it too late. And it would save us all a lot of trouble if we could get a message to him to see sense and come home.'

Inspector Leyton's office was efficiently tidy. He was a non-smoker and the room smelled of air-freshener.

'In my view, all this talk about absconding is so much poppycock. We have the media to thank for that, triggered off by a pack of layabouts up at the college. The evidence they've tried to get us to listen to is just a muddle that proves nothing at all. The thing would be diametrically out of character. The man isn't a seducer, and the girl's a young prude. Moreover, any girl stuck on an older man would want someone a bit dishier than Everard. And I must say this, Mr Kenworthy: if you're going round asking questions that are filling people's heads with fanciful nonsense, you're doing neither us nor the couple any service at all.'

'I'm sorry you take such a jaundiced view of me. They have, after all, both disappeared.'

'Separately. Of that I am in no doubt at all. And in the girl's case, it's serious—though hardly, in this day and age, exceptional. Your ex-colleagues in the Met. are on the ball, and I dare say you have confidence in them, if not in us here. There you have it. I've put my point of view. You're a free agent.'

'But not an irresponsible one. You don't know me. I'd be the last man on earth to risk fouling another man's pitch.'

'It's up to you.'

'I would, of course, undertake nothing without keeping you faithfully posted.'

'I'm sure. And I promise you I will carefully study any memoranda or notes that you care to submit, listen to any view that you want to put forward. But my time *is* limited—'

'Of course. I'll think it over and let you know what I'm going to do. I'm strongly tempted at this moment to go home and continue to spend my mornings listening to Jimmy Young. I've made no promises to Mrs Everard.'

'As I say, it's for you to decide.'

Inspector Leyton was playing it low profile to the end, but his face looked hopeful of the prospect of Kenworthy's withdrawal. Kenworthy got up and left, wishing them a respectable good morning in the public office but aware of the foreignness to him of the whole setup: of the sickening reminders of a world in which he had had so much hope in his early days—the duty rosters, the keenness with which a probationer was taking a telephone call, a burly couple coming out of the CID room with intent to wipe one off the record. Balance that against the corrupt men who had been promoted over his head, against Vice Squad officers helping to edit a porn magazine in Soho, and it wouldn't take him long to be feeling like Everard in the new kind of school. Bugger it! It was a pity that Elspeth had fanned dying embers last night. Well: courtesy demanded that he pay one last call on Blanche Everard.

'Mr Kenworthy?'

It was the youngster on the switchboard, holding the

instrument away from his face on its long flexy cord.

'Yes?'

'Mr Leyton's compliments—and could he ask you to go upstairs again, please? He says it's urgent.'

So Kenworthy made his way back to the upper corridor and found Leyton with files out—and a contrived smile for him this time.

'Sorry about this. Something's blown up that's changed the pattern. I've just had the Met. on. They've found Susan Shires: on a derelict, untended building site between Victoria Street and the river. Dead from multiple injuries. Not many stone's throws from New Scotland Yard.'

'Have they—?'

'Just let me finish this. I'll be with you.'

Leyton was scribbling on an Action slip, which he completed and took to an office a couple of doors away. When he came back, he was clearly minded to be more friendly than before—and unable to conceal a measure of excitement.

'No details are through yet. In any case, it hardly looks as if it's going to be our pigeon at all now. The man who rang was an inspector called Wright. I gather you know him.'

'Know him? I bloody well trained him.'

'Yes. There are one or two stories still current in the force. That's why I mentioned to him that you'd just been in. And he said he wanted to see you—and not tomorrow at that. He should be here in about an hour.'

'Shiner Wright!' Kenworthy said. 'If it's *his* case—'

'Perhaps I might put you a little more fully in the picture,' Leyton started. 'I'm sorry we don't care for private investigators. Maybe you didn't in your time. But Wright said to keep you here at all costs, and that's what I'm doing. And you should know that Susan Shires's suitcase was handed in a few days ago from a sleazy hotel in NW1.

She turned up at this hotel mid-morning, deposited the bag and asked for a double room for one night. And when that raised an eyebrow, she said that she was going to share it with another girl. She turned up at the training college for her interview, seems to have made a good impression on the Vice-Principal. The college is on the southeast outskirts and her appointment was at two o'clock. She was shown round the place and was given a cup of tea by a students' reception committee. She left just before four—the timings are all consonant. But what she didn't do was turn up in NW1 to claim either the room or her case. We do know that she and John Everard left for London on the same train, but it's a popular commuting train, and I see no sinister significance in that. Nor am I inclined to take it as proof of devious intent that they avoided travelling together. My wife and I were once by chance on that train, and we didn't see each other.'

'There are the allegations made by these students,' Kenworthy said. 'Maybe they don't amount to much— and maybe they told me a little more than they told you. I think in your case they set out with the deliberate intention of drumming up misunderstandings. But if it were my business, I'd want to cross-check for the sake of elimination. There were various people on the 8.05 who are quoted as having seen Everard and the girl together: various brothers, fathers, and someone I can't properly place for you, whom they called Dave's mother. The couple are supposed to have met outside the ticket barrier and gone together into the station buffet. Now that doesn't necessarily point to criminal intent. Let's just imagine they meet. They're surprised to see each other. He asks her where she's going and she tells him about her interview. What more natural, since he's her teacher, who's been preparing her for the career she wants, than that he should want to talk to her about her prospects, about the line to take with stock questions in the interview? So they go for a coffee.'

'That makes sense.'

'Then she goes off alone and makes this very strange hotel booking. Can you imagine him saying to her, "This is the chance we've both been waiting for. Let's sleep together. You go to this slummy hotel and book us a room"? If that's what they wanted, then surely to goodness he'd make the arrangements himself—and choose somewhere decent. After all, he was the one with time to spare, and she'd got to get across London. And good God!'

Kenworthy suddenly thumped Leyton's desk.

'The sere, the yellow leaf! I must be in my dotage! What's she doing with a packed suitcase anyway—and overnight things? She's on a journey that she can comfortably do in a day, and there are trains back to Warnford till midnight.'

Leyton rested his chin in his hand, trying to think things to a conclusion while at the same time paying attention to Kenworthy's welter of words.

'In fact we know,' Kenworthy said, 'that she was back in Central London in time to get home. Because Dave's mother saw her again—outside the barrier before the departure of the 5.28. We really will have to send a sergeant to find out who Dave is and go and talk to his Ma. Because she saw them walk together, away from the barrier, and out back into the street. Well? Need that be insidious? When he says goodbye to her in the morning, he says to her, "Look, I'm keen to know how you get on at the interview. Meet me here between five and half past, and we'll go and have a plate of nosh somewhere." '

'Possibly.'

'Don't forget that Everard was the one with the problem of time to be killed.'

'You've said that before. How do you know?'

'Ah!'

And Kenworthy suddenly laughed.

'If only Shiner could hear me, he'd laugh like a drain. The old Kenworthy imagination revving up for take-off again! He used to protect me from it: that was his job as my sergeant. But I'll tell you how I've worked things out. You have my authority to sling office furniture at me if I say anything too bloody stupid. Everard gets off early that morning, because he wants away. He's been planning this for some time, including his admirable accounts and his bag-packing. He doesn't want to be hanging about house or college on the day of departure. So he'll have a day in London. Plenty to do there. Plenty of living it up, of the sort he's been promising himself. And he's on his way to the Continent. I'm pretty sure of that. In fact, I may be on the way there myself, unless Shiner wants it kept strictly for Interpol. In which case I'd have no wish to be locked up in some benighted Schleswig-Holstein nick whilst my bona fides are cleared. Where was I?'

'On the Continent.'

'Yes. A man besotted with trains. So I asked myself, when Mrs Everard first mentioned the thought, which train would he go on? And my first thought was Hook-Night. An admirable train: dawn in Rotterdam, and you can sit in the diner with a damned great plate of ham and eggs, and look at eye-level through the windows of the flats, watch Dutchmen getting ready to go to work, beautiful kitchens, blue-and-white Delft ware, coffee-mills on shelves. Where am I?'

'Rotterdam.'

'Yes. Then I thought, no. A lovely train. But it isn't the one I'd choose. What's the one journey that really evokes the Great Trains of the world?'

'Orient Express.'

'No longer exists. You ought to watch more telly. No. Dunkirk Night Ferry!' Kenworthy practically blazed. 'Sleeping-car attendants in brown uniforms and *képis*, looking as if they were gendarmes who'd stepped out of the old Linguaphone adverts. Of course he'd go Night Ferry Dunkirk. The connoisseur's train.'

'Do you mind if I ask you, Kenworthy—is this how you broke all your big cases?'

'Roughly. And another thought came to me. If he went Night Dunkirk, then Normandy would surely be his first call. So it's Marie-Thérèse Besson who might hold the key.'

Leyton went through the motions of burlesque breathlessness.

'Just a minute. Or two minutes. Or three. Who's Marie-Thérèse Besson? And why Schleswig-Holstein? And what's all this about Everard being a railway buff?'

Kenworthy knew then that the stupid woman had told the police nearly nothing. Perhaps they hadn't exactly encouraged her. Perhaps she hadn't wanted to parade these private things that were highly probably irrelevant. Perhaps she was one of those imbeciles who thought the police could work miracles. Perhaps it was only the later talk with her solicitor that had persuaded her to say everything she thought. Or perhaps it was the way he had himself interviewed her that had loosened her tongue.

Leyton sent for coffee and Kenworthy, returning to placid normality, enlightened him about some of Everard's idiosyncrasies. Then Wright was arriving, a bit broader, shorter-haired, looking slightly more harrassed than when he had been Kenworthy's sergeant. After the vigorous hand-shaking there were some seconds of equally robust laughter, hardly suited to the beginning of a murder enquiry, but suggesting that some of the anxious times of the past were happy ones in retrospect. The hilarity—in which Leyton was no more than a spectator with an unconvincing smile—was interrupted by his telephone, and he was asked if he would take a call from Hunstanton. He listened carefully, looked at first perplexed and then satisfied.

'Ten thousand a year leave house and home,' he said, when he had put down the receiver, 'which makes two hundred a week, give or take a digit or two. And since Mrs Everard stood simpering at the desk sergeant, I've tried to keep track of all the flimsies. A Spanish girl abandoned on Victoria Station. A girl at a gypsy fortune-teller's on a pier. Some London kid who was apparently won on a pintable. A woman in the West Country who saw a respectable man with a tart. Now there's a small-time grass up in Norfolk who says the couple spent last night at a hotel in Hunstanton, and that Everard did not even trouble to deny his identity. The Norfolk police have checked his story and traced the pair back to a pub further round the coast, where they spent the previous night — and Everard left an envelope in the waste bin with his name on it.'

Kenworthy turned to Wright.

'How sure can you be of the identification of the corpse near Victoria?'

'Provisional. Comparison with the photograph, which was less than satisfactory. The body was in a hell of a mess, had been mostly buried under a heap of hardcore. But she had a green tam-o'-shanter, just as the manager of the Euston hotel described. And there were name tags in her clothes — same batch as those in the suitcase. One of the things I am here for, of course, is to take one of her parents to the mortuary. What a bloody job this is!'

'How long's she been dead?'

'Days. That's as near as we can get till the pathologist's finished.'

'So is Everard wandering up and down the East Coast with some other lass? That would surprise me. I was beginning to trust him.'

'Or could somebody have switched the identification hints in Westminster? It looks, by the way, as if the murder may not have taken place there. She may have been dumped.'

And in this maelstrom of introductory impressions, Leyton had yet another idea.

'If you were right, Kenworthy—and my mind's open to anything in this case—'

'Thank you—'

'I didn't mean it that way. What I'm thinking is, if you were right about the Night Ferry to Dunkirk, he might even have told the girl what he was up to, and she might have decided to go and see him off.'

'And you think he might have come back from Dunkirk to Norfolk, do you?'

'What the hell's all this about Dunkirk?' Wright asked.

'Let's all take life quietly for a minute or two, shall we, Shiner? And I'll tell you all about it. And after that, I'll shut up. Don't be afraid of reminding me that I'm working for you for a change.'

CHAPTER 11

Husum, on the North Sea coast of the West German province of Schleswig, is a town of the sea, but not always visibly so, separated as it is from the breakers by a dreary panorama of parallel (and historic) sea walls. The nineteenth-century poet Theodor Storm was born there and perpetuated its migrant geese and the omnipresent voice of the sea; less resonant than a roar, more soul-searing than a sibilance, it is a difficult sound to describe. Storm used the word *Brausen*; which the dictionary translates as rage; which is inadequate. It is a sound that never stops, so that even in November, when the cold mists obscure even the nearest street-corner, nobody doubts that the sea is still there. The inhabitants of

Husum have listened to the *Brausen* for so long that they are no longer aware of it. But they would wonder what had happened if it ever stopped.

Lieselotte Garn (Mölling, as Blanche Everard had referred to her to Kenworthy, was her name by her first marriage) was as inured to the *Brausen* as any other Husumite, but she was conscious of a rushing in her ears when she recognized Jack Everard's handwriting in the morning post. It was a decade since their correspondence had fallen off. Jack Everard did not even know her second married name.

And now he was coming to see her, even gave a precise date, some three weeks hence. She was not, as they say, at all sanguine about it.

Lieselotte Garn had developed into a comfortable *Hausfrau*, if the notion of comfort can be applied to physiological upholstery so ample as to induce bronchial symptoms on the slightest exertion. She had been slender—indeed, at first actually hungry—when Jack had first pulled strings to get her a flat to which she had no entitlement whatever. And she had been intense: about war-guilt, about Borchert and Kafka, authors whom Jack had helped her to discover. She was still intense, but it was mostly these days about domestic matters.

She did not want Everard to come. Paul Werner Garn was given to blind fits of jealousy, even about things so enshrouded in the past that they offered no threat to his security. She had told her new husband all about Everard; and his face had taken on that look of bewilderment and hurt that could keep her awake at nights. He seemed to think that there was some magic of cosmic mathematics—some quirk of relativity perhaps—that enabled him to possess her in the past as he did in the present. She did not want Paul Werner even to be reminded of the existence of Jack Everard, let alone have to play the *korrekt* host to him.

But Everard told her in his letter precisely when he proposed to start out on his travels. He was already on his way, and there was no address at which she could write to him to put him off.

Marie-Thérèse Besson's house, in yellow and white brick, stood on one of the right bank hillsides, overlooking the Seine between Caudebec en Caux and Villequier. She called it a *château*, for which label it had threshold qualifications, though neighbours had been known to pass cynical comments.

In the forepart of the morning, Marie-Thérèse Besson bore only a remote resemblance to the coiffed, manicured and *soigné* figure known as Emma to Everard's irreverent colleagues. But her *toilette* was leisurely, regular and adroit; it took a good hour, these days, for her pots, bowls and wig-box to make good the ravages of sleep.

Unlike Lieselotte Garn, she was in no way distressed to receive Everard's letter. She saw him, after all, at least twice most years, and there was often a query or request in the post about some aspect of his perpetual logistics.

She telephoned Lefèvre and asked him to try to get her a *jambon d'Espagne*. She knew how much Everard liked it.

The Gänsergrundl is a steep valley in the Zillertal Alps, down which the Zepter brook runs down past the village of Brach into the Mergelspeicher reservoir. There is a cluster of farms and a hotel or two down in the valley bottom, but very few new faces are seen after mid autumn. The terrain is too rough and rock-strewn for skiing, and by November the snow lies thick over the Gänsejoch, the Bracherbubl and the Zepterspitze: the landmarks that serve the summer tourists who follow the hikers' numbered footpath into Italy.

The Gasthof Zum Weissen Bock was the only hostelry

that had remained open this month, and that only for such guests as had a novel to write, or were content to spend most of their day looking out from the overheated bar at the frozen slopes.

There is a miniature bay between Blakeney and the village of Weybourne which is drawn to the traveller's attention by a crooked fingerpost lettered *Beach*. It was on the sands of this bay that Alice Bayne, a widow of a certain age, unleashed Caesar, her affectionate and intelligent Airedale terrier.

Effusive in its liberty, the dog rushed off almost witlessly in various successive directions. He did not care for the sea itself, in which his mistress took an equally witless pleasure in seeing him immersed. Eventually he followed some mystic trail to a declivity in the dunes where he began to scrabble frenziedly.

It was only a matter of seconds before he unearthed a human foot, whereupon Alice Bayne screamed. Then she picked up a green tam-o'-shanter that was lying in the sand near where the body might have a head.

CHAPTER 12

Kenworthy was resolute about one thing: the old days were gone, and he was Shiner's subordinate.

But there were times when he almost forgot this, and it took a good deal of repetitious persuasion, perilously close to nagging, to get Shiner to see that one of their early calls must absolutely be on a gypsy fortune-teller who went by the professional name of Rosanna.

When they got there—and a lot of valuable time went by the board in reaching the Norfolk coast—he tried Shiner's patience further by insisting that the interview take place in the booth on the pier.

'I want it to be where she talked to the girl. That way she'll remember things she might otherwise forget.'

Shiner went to fetch Rosie-Anne from her semi on the outskirts of town, whilst Kenworthy stood in the lee of the children's helter-skelter and looked moodily down into the sea.

Rosie-Anne took no pleasure in being drawn out into a November north-easterly, and no consolation from the fact that her disturbers were the police. Nor was she joyous when Kenworthy told her he wanted his palm read.

'Listen,' she said, her Bradford vowels flat and unhappy, 'I know the law as well as you do, as far as it affects my job, and you can't get me under the Vagrancy Act, because I'm not a vagrant. Why the hell should I read your palm?'

'For two quid?'

Kenworthy peeled off two notes and handed them to her, telling Wright to be sure not to forget to put them down as expenses. He held out his hand.

'You're not serious?'

'Just tell me what you see there.'

The woman looked at him with deep-rooted distrust.

The electrician had finished his work about the kiosk. There were fresh drill-holes in the woodwork, shavings spilled over a sill. Nothing had been cleared up, perhaps wouldn't be till the eve of next Easter. Through the gaps between the floor timbers they could hear and see the tide lapping round the piles.

She had no idea at all whether she ought to take him at his word or not, looked down at his palm for a moment as if she had decided to.

'Just treat me as if I were the Archduke of Rumptsi-Bumptsi.'

'Listen: those testimonials in the window are genuine.'

'I know. I wouldn't be here if I didn't believe in you.'

It was nearly enough to do the trick. She took his hand uncertainly by the wrist.

'Just tell me what you see there.'

'I see a big office building at night. Lights are on on all floors—Oh, this is plain stupid.'

'Yes, isn't it? Shall I tell you what it's all about?'

Kenworthy's smile would have disarmed more uneasy consciences than Rosie-Anne's.

'Gypsy Rosanna: I know how you people work. You're detectives; more effective than some I have known in the force in my time. The Line of Life, the Mount of Jupiter: that's all secondary stuff. You look at people, weigh them up, do a bit of preliminary chatting, get them to let slip odd little things about themselves. Then when you get on to the magic, you can stick to what's probable. You tell them, in fact, things it will please them to hear. It's an art. You have it worked out. I respect you for it.'

'It's strictly for amusement only,' she said self-defensively.

'But you wouldn't be able to sell it as amusement, if you were regularly too far off-beam.'

'There's no trickery in it,' she said.

'Stop trying to spoil it, Rosie-Anne. You're not being got at.'

'What are you after?' she asked.

'The couple who came here that day you were having the rewiring done. I want to know all you can tell me about them.'

'Oh—them?'

It was clear she had something uneasy in her memory. She did not look happy to be asked.

'Let's start at the beginning. You'll have read of this schoolmaster who's supposed to have been roaming the country with one of his pupils. Was it them?'

'I have wondered—since. There hadn't been anything

in the papers about them before this pair came. And I can't be sure. The pictures you put out were so out of date. A girl grows up quickly. And I really didn't see all that much of the man, what with his scarf up round his chin. And he never really turned to face me.'

'We have the originals here. A bit less smudgy, at any rate, than those in the press. Perhaps you'd like to refresh your memory.'

But when she had seen them, she was still too uncertain to commit herself.

'Just tell me anything that comes into your mind, then.'

'She was unhappy.'

'And under some compulsion to consult her fates? Do you think she believed in witchcraft and sorcery?'

'No. Not more than most people. But I know how this comes about. I'm always worried when someone comes in who might be going to take it too seriously. You see, people get upset. They have something on their mind. They wish someone would make it up for them. They cotton on to any little thing that they think might be the writing on the wall. It's like the horoscopes in the paper. People don't really believe them. But if it says "Wear bright colours on Tuesday," there are people who won't take a chance. I don't mind that so much. That's just fun-forecasting. But I hate to see a certain type come in through that door. There's always the chance that I might mean too much to them. I have to be very careful indeed.'

'And you were careful with this girl?'

'Very.'

'Tell us what put you off.'

'The man, chiefly—or in the first place. He thought she was wasting her own time and his, coming in here. And he was grumpy about it. Then she was wearing a wedding-ring so loose that I could see it had never been custom-bought for her. She even took it off for her com-

fort, while I looked at her hand. I started off by telling
her she was a long way from home, hoping she'd volun-
teer something. But when I got a bit careless in the way I
was putting things, she came the acid with me — more
acid than I'd have thought, from her age and her general
appearance. "I'm paying to ask the questions", she said.'
    'Intelligent?'
    'More than she looked.'
    'Anything else about her.'
    'Drugs.'
    'You mean the usual symptoms? Shaky? Slurred
speech?'
    'No. Marks up her arm. Not rough, the way you some-
times see them up the hippies' wrists. These looked as if
they'd been done by somebody who knew what he was
about.'
    'Did you say anything about them, directly or indirectly?'
    'No. I thought perhaps I ought to: you know, perhaps
say something about avoiding unnatural things. And then
I thought, it was best not to upset her. She was on edge.
She'd had one little go at me. I didn't want hysterics. I
decided I'd keep it as short as I could, while still giving
her her money's worth. So I stuck to the harmless stuff. I
said a lot of things, really, that were intended to cheer her
up: glowing future — all that.'
    'And did she cheer up?'
    'No. She was past it. I wished I could have done
something to help — but what? You can't go dialling 999
because you've come across someone unhappy, can you?'
    'No. More's the pity — except that I wouldn't care to be
manning the switchboard.'

Wright and Kenworthy walked back along the pier at a
pace dictated by the wind, from which immediate shelter
was indicated. Gypsy Rosanna remained behind in her
booth, determined to clear up the electrician's mess

before she set eyes on the place again.

'So?' Wright said. 'We're further forward, are we? We're clear now on the identification in Victoria: Susan Shires. The pathologist can't work wonders: but she seems to have died the day she left home. She'd had a massive overdose of lysergic acid: LSD to the layman. There's no report of this other couple in Norfolk till the day after that. There's Everard's envelope in a waste bin. There's Hunstanton, and this common informer who claims that Everard offered him a bribe not to give him away. There's the body on the beach, attacked with furious strength, asphyxiated with her head in a plastic bag; and a green tam-o'-shanter in the sand. Has Everard some fetish about green tam-o'-shanters? We haven't identified the corpse. Where did he pick her up? Who will he pick up next, if he already hasn't? All forces, particularly East Anglian, are running the rule over any middle-aged man seen about with an adolescent girl.'

'I'm sure you've got everything possible laid on, Shiner. So that all that your middle-aged man has to do, if he's any sense, is not to be seen out and about in the company of girls. If he can discipline himself to do that, you'll have a job finding him. A case of some complexity.'

'Some.'

'You're forgetting the greatest complexity of all.'

'And what's that?'

'Why does an uncolourful, biddable, some might say positively angelic young lady carry a bag that she does not need, to a hotel that is not her scene, to book a room that she does not use?'

'That's a question that we're not going to answer till the last ditch, Simon.'

'I disagree, Shiner. I disagree profoundly.'

They had at last reached Wright's car, and Kenworthy was doing his best to arrange his legs in the confined space.

'I just don't quite get that last one, Simon.'

'The last ditch? Until we know why she booked at that hotel, we shan't know where to look for the last ditch.'

'I don't quite see what you mean.'

'It's a question of cart before horse, Shiner. Which is cart and which is horse? Until we know that, we can't start looking for who killed Sue Shires.'

'Oh, God, Simon—'

'I don't think it's going to be all that difficult—at the last ditch. I dare say Everard can tell us.'

'Who was it said cart before horse? First find Everard—'

'Oh, Shiner, Shiner, Shiner—whatever has happened to your faith? Haven't I said I will find him for you? If I can get a first-class sleeper tonight, I shall be on my way to Austria. I no longer think he'd put Normandy first.'

Wright sighed heavily.

'Remember how I went on, Shiner, about Everard's preference for Dover-Dunkirk? For reasons that I went into in front of a not very appreciative Leyton, I'm essentially a Harwich-Hook man myself.'

Wright drove a mile in silence.

'You've done this to me before, Simon.'

'What's that, lad?'

'Got to the stage where you know the answer, but it's so damned outrageous that you sit tight on it.'

'I have no more information at my disposal than you have.'

'I suppose it's another case of that bloody imagination of yours. One of these days you are going to trip up.'

'Have you ever known that happen yet?'

'No, you damned old twister. Because you always keep your mouth shut till you *know* you're right.'

CHAPTER 13

So how would he come? Hire car? Long-distance bus? Lieselotte Garn had had a sleepless night, dreams and waking alike suffused by the *Brausen*, the ceaseless pounding of the waves, the unplaceable seething that never let Husum alone.

For days now she had been on the terrible brink of preparing Paul Werner for their visitor, until the words she rehearsed were buffeting her brain as if they were the North Sea itself. And she continued to fight shy of the confrontation, until fighting shy became itself a torture. To make matters worse, Paul Werner had been for days on end as placid as she had ever known him; not exactly like a cat that purrs, but like one that does not whimper, does not spit at harmless shadows, does not scratch doors or claw at precious hangings.

Of course, he would come by train. He would fly to Hamburg and then take the West Coast route. He had always been crazy about trains. He had had six books, that he said he had had in his kit-bag all through the war, and one of them was an English Railway Guide that she had seen him pore over for hours.

They had been happy days, haunted throughout only by the knowledge that they were not going to last. He had been kind to her, kinder than she had ever known a man; clever—and so quiet. So quiet that she had always told him that his cleverness would never stand a chance. Yet he could be shrewd, too. A saintly man—who never tried to preach his saintliness over into the lives of others. Saintly: but there had been nothing saintly about the fiddle he had operated with the *Opfer des Fascismus*, the bureau that recompensed Nazi victims, in order to get her a flat: get *them* a flat. There had been long evenings when they had not talked much, hadn't wanted to make love—though when they did that, their unity had rocked out of this world. Often enough, they hadn't wanted to go anywhere, hadn't wanted to do anything, except be together, in the same room, in opposite corners, one or the other of them looking up after an interval to see the other, then bend back over the reading, the sewing, the report or the letter that was being quietly written.

She tried to guess which train he would come by: there were several possibilities. She picked on one, arbitrarily, and then was certain that this would be the one, as if, in the absence of telepathy, she was forcing a telepathic certainty on herself. She would go down, and do some idle shopping in the neighbourhood of the station at the right time, run into him casually, head him off, tell him to stay at the Stadt am Meer or the Thomas, where she would find her way to him if and when circumstances permitted.

She was out too soon, giving herself too much time, began to have difficulty in spinning out her loitering by shop windows, had to prevaricate with two neighbours eager for coffee and cakes; heard the train; went on loitering for some time after all the obvious passengers had come out into the street. He was not on the train; or the next; or on any train that day; or the next day—or the next—

Marie-Thérèse Besson wondered what Monsieur Everard was up to. He was a strange man. Sometimes she thought that the long evenings together, which seemed to have become an immovable feast two or three times a year, were going to last for ever, that the clock had stopped, that the *château* on the hillside was rolling round the firmament in a darkness that was going to know no more dawn. He was so dull; and his dullness seemed to have intensified itself with the passing of the years that she had known him. He was correct; yes; she would not have to do with a man who was not correct. But there were times when correctness could become leaden. And yet there were times when she caught him looking at her covertly, as if—

No; he couldn't be so stupid; and, *bon Dieu*, she did not want the burden of seeking for charitable ways of fobbing off *that*—

His letters, though, were a different thing. She always eagerly opened his letters. His French was pedantic, grammatically faultless, occasionally studded with some archaism that made her want to titter. But he was capable of turning an elegant antithesis, not beyond a witty play on words. Even his business letters were worth reading for their own sake.

And his business letters were reliable, too; so prompt, so unambiguous; so much like the sort of work that the uncompromising teacher demands from the perfect class.

She often wondered how any thread of variety could ever enter his life with that desiccated, desperately un-whimsical wife he had brought with him one year. Two such people might well have been made for each other, but their sum total would sink in a sea of mercury.

It was odd, though, this last letter—a business letter— so lit up by the news that he was coming, a visit out of time, a gift from his gods, train and local bus times exactly stated.

Odd that he hadn't arrived; or written to apologize.

They had considerable difficulty in understanding the Englishman in the Gasthof Zum Weissen Bock at Brach. They liked him, as they liked any orderly guest who paid in advance, thanked them profusely after every meal and kept out of their way in the public rooms when they were cleaning. He was always polite, if less than warm, spoke German well; but no one seemed able to penetrate the surface. And the least penetrable thing about him was what he was here for at all. He was not, like Fräulein Kornahl, writing a novel; he did not drink rumbustiously, like Herr Francke and Herr Giebel. He certainly did like his beer, but he went sparingly at it, in a way that clearly showed he was watching each *Groschen*. He went out occasionally, if snow was not actually falling, but they had all — guests, management and staff — noticed his unwillingness ever to walk *with* anyone. Sometimes one of them had fallen in step with him, when they met by the reservoir, or on the footpath by the Zepterbach. But he had somehow, without ever showing the slightest trace of rudeness, shown that he wanted to throw them off. Olga, who looked after his room, said that he kept a fantastic range of pills up there.

When he did go out walking, he would content himself with a couple of hundred yards, just as far as the snow was cleared, and usually in the same direction, peering up at the Gänsejoch, asking questions sometimes about that footpath. How far was it before you came to the *Zollwarthütte*, the frontier-post? Did Italy look any different from this? How could it look different? It was still the Tirol, wasn't it — had ding-donged between overlords more than once in the course of history?

Then there was his attitude to Fräulein Kornahl: a strange woman, everyone had thought at first, but not in that neurotic sense in which artists and aesthetes were often withdrawn from society. She ate well, enjoyed her aperitifs and kept her own bottle of wine, a gratifyingly chosen Elsasser Gewurztraminer, which was brought to her evening table. She knew what was going on in the world about her, called all the members of the guest-house staff by their Christian names, walked for an hour a day and wrote for four, in the winter-sunniest window-seat. Nor was there about her anything of the caricature of the muse-lorn. God knows how old she was, but she knew how not to look it: a supple, slender but not angular figure, with blonde, glossily waved hair that wasn't her own, but that suited her. Some thought that she had never been married, others that she had been widowed or divorced, some that she had always enjoyed herself, but that takers were not so easy to come by these days. *Die grosse Anna*, the cook, who saw all she saw through a crack in the door, but who was nevertheless a sorceress's wellspring of arcane information (occasionally proved right) said that she was of Slav origin, and that her original name had been Kornalewski.

Be all that as it may, there were refreshing signs that the Englishman was interested in her. The Gasthof Zum Weissen Bock loved a lover, not perhaps with the extravagance of Gladys Turnbull, but at any rate with the feeling that it brought life to the place to have something going on in it out of season. Hence it was lost on no one that his eyes often moved in her direction at supper-time. In fact, at the end of his first week, he invited himself to have his coffee served at her table, and the next night she came over to his. But then they remained apart for two evenings, and the suggestion seemed never to have been made by either of them that they should actually eat together. It was as if he were a man under some inner compulsion to put up barriers between himself and obvious courses of action; though he himself would doubtlessly have put it down as proper respect for the privacy of others.

Then came the afternoon when he had been for a longer walk than usual, and in the opposite direction from the one that he usually took, along the cleared road by the reservoir lake, and into the pine fringes of the Neukedarwald. Franz Giebel and Putzi Francke had been down to Mayrhofen for shopping and lunch and had come back with a special treat for him, a three-day old copy of the London *Times*. He accepted this enthusiastically, and with an offer of money that was declined — and retired at once into a corner with the crossword. But later he delved into its news pages and it was not long before he was showing duly reported signs of extreme distraction. He knocked over a glass of water on his supper-table, hopelessly mistook some subject of conversation that his waitress tried to open up with him — and frustrated the efforts of Hilde Kornahl (abandoned after the third attempt) to catch his eye. He was seen studying the instructions on the International pages of the telephone directory; but no action actually arose out of that.

A couple of days later another Englishman arrived, unheralded and uncertain at first whether to stay overnight or not. He did not ask for Herr Everard, but rapidly found him, and they talked for a long time together in the conservatory. Herr Everard was nervous at first, then confidentially voluble — and finally heartily friendly over the evening meal that they shared. And after that they drank together with a gusto and ill wisdom such as neither of them could have indulged in since their youth. The Gasthof Zum Weissen Bock, inspired by a single integrated spirit, confidently expected both gentlemen to remain siege-bound in their rooms until at least midmorning. And, indeed, Herr Everard did not appear till after eleven and found, apparently, even rolls and butter offensive to his gastronomic imagination. The new Englishman, however, appeared ready to breakfast before anyone was up to serve him; though it did not go unnoticed that he was making a conscious effort to face the day with an appearance of aplomb.

The gentleman filled in his waiting time by letting himself out of the guesthouse and walking a little way up to the track towards the Gänsejoch: the path that so fascinated his friend. He reached a higher point than Herr Everard had ever been known to attain, but of course had to turn back because of the drifting. He was away, hiring a *Droschke* down to Mayrhofen before Herr Everard was up—and promising that he would be back here with his wife, perhaps in the coming spring.

The staff of the Zum Weissen Bock settled down to something like its normal tenor, having debated the transient Englishman with interest. One section of opinion was convinced that he must be some kind of policeman. Some scented international intrigue and *die grosse Anna* believed that Fräulein Kornalewski's antecedents had caught up with her at last.

Things were not quite the same in the guesthouse. Herr Everard had become permanently restless, and though this did not make him irritable with the servants—nor change the rhythm of his contacts with Hilde Kornahl—it affected the guesthouse in an uneasy way. The corporate spirit of the house liked guests to be and seem happy; and Herr Everard therefore became a disturbing presence.

CHAPTER 14

Kenworthy took the expensive evening meal on the train from Munich to Hoek mainly for the sake of the diversion. As far as concerned his outpourings to Inspector Leyton, he had been right about the joys of the Hook-Night route: the blocks of early morning flats in Rotterdam had been as evocative as ever. But Rotterdam is very few minutes distance from the Hook; and the journey to the Dutch coast from Munich takes all of sixteen hours. Moreover, the afternoon is spent rumbling through the maize fields of the Palatinate, looking at unenchanting villages strung out at intervals amid the red soil. The Rhine gorge is already invisible in the winter evening darkness, and after Cologne the train is chopped into

worm segments to be shunted about the no longer cred-
ible affluence of the Ruhr. It is a train of changed personality, spayed, emasculated, either or both, as it halts
for the benighted oblivion of Kaldenkirchen and
Deventer. By the time it has reached the littoral of
Holland, it is reduced to a mere two or three coaches,
dismally bearing some theoretical connection with the
Essex port of Harwich.

Kenworthy was in a dismal frame of mind as they rattled
past the diabolical retorts of Schiedam. He read his notes
for the last time and put them away.

John Everard had read the news of his alleged elopement with Susan Shires a few days previously in an old
copy of the London *Times*. He had read the definitive
statement that the police were anxious to interview him
and had no doubt, initially, that Kenworthy was the forward scout of the final pincers. He had quietly, firmly,
protested his innocence. And the one quasi-official act
that Kenworthy had performed was to ask to see his
passport. The rectangular imprint of the *Sûreté
Nationale* of the *Gare du Nord* showed that he had arrived
in France when he said he had: early in the morning after
the night when the girl had been killed. Kenworthy had
divined some things correctly: he had travelled Wagons-
Lits via Dunkirk, which meant that he must have been on
Victoria Station between ten and half past on the night in
question. This all but let him out of suspicion of the girl's
murder, but not conclusively so. Kenworthy's notes of this
phase contained a large number of marginal question
marks.

The pathologist could not be expected to perform
miracles of timing about the girl's death. It seemed fairly
certain that she had been with Everard in North London
a little before 5.28. Did this give Everard time to have
done it? If so, where could he possibly have done it? Was
it an acceptable possibility? He was a heart case, suffering

from angina pectoris. He was a mild man, who abhorred violence, and there was no record or suggestion of sexual aberration. And the girl's body was said to have been overcharged with LSD. Was this something to do with him? Surely Susan wasn't an addict? Had he slipped it to her underhand, then? Was that what he called living it up, reacting against the disciplines of a life-time? Had he, in short, gone mad? Could he, within the space of a few hours, have drugged her and killed her? Was she too far under the influence to give an account of herself in defence? And then had he, a heart case, recovered sufficiently from all this physical and emotional exhaustion to have cleaned himself up and transported the corpse through a busy area, at a by no means deserted hour of night? And got himself to the Dunkirk Night Ferry comfortably and calmly on time?

Kenworthy might reasonably have been expected to ring Shiner at this stage, at least to tell him that Everard was found. But he didn't. It was a joy, being a freelance. God knows what margin of liberty and irresponsibility he might still find to expand into.

At least Everard was now exonerated from all that had been going on in East Anglia. He could not be the man who had played fruit machines, hung about on a wintry pier, initiated a virgin at the Coastguard and suffocated a girl in the sand. Even less could the girl in the sand, green tam-o'-shanter or not, have been Susan Shires, already dead.

But Kenworthy had continued to be liberal with his question marks. It had been known, increasingly since the eased frontiers of EEC, for a man to walk past a barrier with his passport unstamped. Usually this was fortuitous — but were there ways in which a man could make sure it happened? Could Everard have got back to England, hired a car and gone motoring up the Norfolk coast with someone he had picked up? And then come

back to Brach? The question was hardly worth the ballpoint ink: if only in face of the evidence of the staff and
other guests at the Zum Weissen Bock and the registration slip filed with the Austrian police; though a purist
might have argued that there could have been complex
collusion, and the registration could have been fiddled by
the guesthouse at its own risk.

And what had happened to the two vague women in
Everard's life? Why had he called off his plan to go swanning over the North German plain up to Husum? Was it
because, in the cold reality of the final moment, he saw
that there could be no future for him with Lieselotte? He
had told Kenworthy that he had suddenly realized that
she belonged as inextricably as anyone else to that very
past that he wanted to slough off. So did Marie-Thérèse
Besson: what had he in common with her, other than that
she spoke French and knew more than he did about some
of the books that he received a County Council salary to
teach?

A good deal of unpalatable, harsh, black and white
truth had come to Everard, so he said, on that far from
idealized train journey. He had been woken by the clank-
ing chains of the Dunkirk Night Ferry as they embarked,
shunted, cast off and berthed. He had lain awake looking
at the parks of massive articulated container lorries, mar-
shalled under the floodlights of quaysides that belonged,
not to romance, but to economics.

The final puncture in his deflation had been the discovery of something that his own limping intelligence
should have told him: that the footpath to Italy was closed,
that it would have to be an early and felicitous spring that
enabled him to struggle over the Gänsejoch in less than
five months from now.

The only thing that he had achieved was his escape
from the Sixth Form College; and he was unchanged by
his liberty. He was still the man he had been before the

shades of the twentieth-century bridewell had closed
round him.

Live it up?

Live what up?

Take Hilde Kornahl: beckoning, giving him the green-
est of green lights; a physically attractive, discerning
woman, a creative spirit not to be scorned (she had let
him read a few pages of her work), an intellectual companion worth crossing a few frontiers to find.

But he was no more capable of sleeping with her than
he had been of sleeping with the first girl he had fallen in
love with in puberty.

Had he needed Blanche, then?

Now all he could do was scribble sums on scraps of
paper in his bedroom twice a week, working out how long
he could string out his Austrian schillings, calculating
how many days and weeks of Gasthof life he must subtract
for a half-bottle of wine or a litre of beer. The same
applied to his diminishing store of drugs. He had been
stockpiling them for months, not without an occasional
showing of guile in the doctor's dispensary, building up
his store from the moment when it first looked as if
Operation *Crève-Coéur* was closing in on him. They
could not last for ever. What then? Betake himself to an
Austrian doctor, with the risk of finding himself in the
channels that led home? Or which might make appalling
inroads into his funds? Or simply die? He had lost his taste
for dying, too: even for dying dramatically, on the edge of
a mule track that led to the poet's land of lemon trees.

It had taken time for Kenworthy to nurture Everard's
confidence. A *Stein* or two of the excellent Austrian ale
had contributed substantially to the process. And Kenworthy had talked about himself a good deal more than
he had ever intended at the outset: about the sickness of
his own late environment; about what it felt like to see
something brought into disrepute that you had once

believed in, something that had been both the form and content of your life. Everard had slowly come to accept that Kenworthy was a friend. Both men had drunk more—and with greater gusto—than either had allowed himself to do for years. The beer was bodisome and bitter; the ambience—the *Stimmung*, the Austrians called it—was benign: red warmth glowing through the mica doors of a monumental tiled stove; antlers and oil paintings of Alpine valley watermills against the seasoned panelling. Kenworthy had often been conscious, in his working years, of playing on false trust; of playing the soul-mate to a man who, any minute now, was going to be tricked into betraying himself.

Yet now he felt, as the capillary veins thickened gratifyingly about his nostrils and lips, as if he might be the one who was being strung along, lulled into the illusion that he was keeping sympathetic company.

'I wonder you didn't run into Susan Shires yourself. She did go to London that day. She could well have been on the same train.'

'She *was* on the same train. I didn't see her till we were both through the barrier. There's nothing surprising in that.'

'Of course not.'

'I was surprised to see her there. I knew she was a candidate for training college entrance, but I'd no detailed knowledge of what stage she'd got to. And there were a lot of things I wanted to tell her, when I heard she was going to St Bart's. She was offering modern languages as a main subject, and I knew the lecturer who would be interviewing her: Don Cavenham. He has a predilection for the byroads of French seventeenth-century literature—men like Théophile de Viau. I thought it would be a good idea to tip her off about his likes and dislikes. So I suggested a coffee. We went into the buffet.'

Fräulein Kornahl came into the room and sat down in a

corner far removed from them, well out of earshot. She ordered a small and essentially local liqueur, perhaps for the joy of the play of the light in its gentian violet depths.

'It was ironical,' Everard said. 'Here was I, putting all this behind me, and suddenly getting as enthusiastic as ever about a pupil's fortunes. I have—let's say *had*—a headmaster who spends nine tenths of his time talking about involvement. Well, I've never been able to work without involvement, though mine isn't the same type as his. I was involved in Susan Shires's interview, and I suddenly didn't want to go off into the unknown without knowing the outcome of it. It doesn't make sense, does it? Perhaps I mean that I wanted *her* to know that *I* was interested. So I said that I'd meet her back at the station, between five and half-past, because I'd time on my hands. And we did meet, and she was over the moon about the way the interview had gone.'

Kenworthy looked at Everard's flushed face, his schoolboyish frankness.

'It was a peculiar place to meet, though, in the afternoon, wasn't it, the terminus?'

'Not really. I didn't think Susan knew London too well, and I was quite happy to come up that way again later in the day. There was an exhibition of railway posters that I wanted to fit in.'

'That's not what I mean. I mean: you *knew*, surely, that she wasn't going back to Warnford that night.'

It all turned on the girl's suitcase. Wright had raised that key question when he had taken Susan's parents— they had both insisted on going—to the mortuary for the identification. Had they known that she had taken a night's things away with her—on a day trip?

But of course they did. There were other old girls from the school at Bart's Training College, and sometimes a student up for interview would be invited to stay the night—if there happened to be a guest-room vacant.

Sometimes a shake-down was arranged in a friend's bedroom. Susan had hoped that something like that would happen. At least, if it did, she'd be ready.

Kenworthy looked keenly at Everard.

'That was just one of those silly things,' Everard said. 'That morning, in the buffet, we made the afternoon rendezvous, and then for the first time I noticed what sort of a case it was she had with her. I made some silly joke about it: asked her if she was going to camp in Bart's grounds. And she said, no, but she wasn't going home to Warnford that evening. She was taking advantage of being in town to go and see *Jesus Christ Superstar*. And she'd stay the night, because it would be a rush to catch the last train, which is often unpleasantly full of drunks.'

'Go to the theatre and spend the night at a hotel—alone?'

'Oh, no. There were one or two of her friends coming up from Warnford after school. We're so near to London, you know: theatres and concerts aren't exactly a safari for a sixth form college.'

'Which friends?'

'I didn't think to ask.'

And then, as Kenworthy's silence made Everard aware of the weakness of that reply, he said helplessly, 'I didn't think to ask. Why should I? I wasn't particularly interested. If you asked me now, I dare say I could guess who'd be in the party.'

'I *am* asking you now.'

'Mary Gallon, Brenda Thwaites, Lucy Turner: Sue's little set.'

'So really you took her a good deal out of her way, bringing her back to the terminus?'

Everard spread his hands in a gesture of futility.

'How can I explain? I don't think my brain was working at top speed. We joked about her suitcase *à propos* of something else. We'd already arranged the afternoon meeting. We'd parted before it suddenly occurred to me that it wasn't a sensible arrangement.'

'You could so easily have gone to see the posters that morning, while you were still in the Marylebone neighbourhood.'

'In the normal course of events, that is what I had proposed to do.'

He suddenly became agitated.

'Surely you don't think I was up to something untoward with Sue that afternoon? Have you never tripped up, made some ambiguous or stupid arrangement with someone, and then not been able to get in touch with them to put it right?'

'Frequently,' Kenworthy said. 'Usually with my wife.'

He forced himself to make notes before falling asleep. There was a distinct working disadvantage in not having the discipline of a report to write for a superior. He had to explain to no one, for example, why he felt sure that Everard was not lying.

But hadn't Susan Shires been at least a little disingenuous?

CHAPTER 15

The night after Kenworthy's departure, Everard was in the state where nothing but another beer could restore his assaulted system. He went into the bar and Hilde Kornahl was there, alone, but not with a liqueur this time: a glass of light white wine: an indigenous *Trifalter*. She beckoned him to her table, making none of that allowance for temperamental rigidity that usually marked their relations with each other.

'Your friend's gone?'

'This morning. He must have caught the post-bus. I'm

afraid I missed him.'

He said this with a touch of shame-face, but Fräulein Kornahl was not one to regard an occasional alcoholic excess as a sin against her Creator.

'You certainly appeared to be enjoying yourselves,' she said.

'I believe I may ultimately recover.'

He ordered his *Stein* and the waitress, as she swung it down to the ancient table, carved with the initials of a century of celebrants, beamed on him as if the Gasthof Zum Weissen Bock was seeing its children brought together at last.

'You'll forgive my asking,' Fräulein Kornahl said. 'But your friend—please don't think I'm trying to lift lids that don't concern me—but I found him fascinating—at a distance. I could hardly break in on you. But people fascinate me, you know. I'm a writer. People are what my millstones need.'

'A policeman,' he said, with enough note of apology for one to be accepted if one were needed. 'No longer active. And not, as far as I know the breed, a characteristic one.'

'A policeman? My word, that would stir up some theories for *die grosse Anna*. A friend from your younger years, I suppose?'

Hilde Kornahl seemed to have discarded most of her rings and bangles this evening. Her fingers looked younger than usual. There was a sense of perfect physical preservation about her, as if a moment of her early maturity had been isolated and held in serenity. Her cheeks had a glaze like Dresden faïence.

'Not at all. He had an unhealthy interest in my immediate past,' he said, not at all considering the consequences of confession.

There was in fact no point at which he actually decided to plunge into autobiography—and certainly no understanding that it was Hilde Kornahl who was calling the tune. But autobiography was what began at that moment: including some features that he was not conscious of ever having previously worked out for himself. He told her what he had read in German literature for his degree, and as he talked, he saw for the first time clearly within himself what it had been like, as a provincial Oxbridge meritocrat, discovering what rarefied heights of scholarship the public schoolboys — the top cream of them, at any rate — had achieved even before they came up as undergraduates.

He talked about his early army days, was properly coy about his phase in counter-intelligence (which, at its most effective, had been concerned with strictly local denazification). He recaptured, and tried to analyse afresh as he talked, the unexpected hours of peace he had found in the incessant *Brausen* of Husum. He enthused about the literally thousands of children to whom he had offered their first experience of wanderlust. He said very little about Marie-Thérèse Besson, whom he now saw as an unsatisfying, bleakly unexotic creature, a chance discovery against a not very enlivening backcloth, her distinction largely a product of his own fancy.

He remembered and dutifully retailed lyrical moments in his own courtship and marriage. Hilde Kornahl did not respond. He called for another *Stein*; she had barely put her lips to her own glass.

He told her why he was here: Operation *Crève-Coeur*. She inclined her head to show her understanding of the mechanics of it; was clearly reserving her judgement on its other aspects. He told her why Kenworthy had come, opened his wallet and showed her the cutting from *The Times*.

'The least of your worries,' she said. 'That man Kenworthy looked to me like the right type to sort the nonsense out of that mess. But you've made mistakes, you know. I'm sorry — it isn't for me to pontificate. I've made mistakes of my own in my time.'

'I'd be grateful to know what you think.'

'How bad's your heart?'

'No worse than it's been for some years. It was bad some weeks before I came away. I really did think I'd reached the last phase. I don't know how I got across London. I had a bad attack when Kenworthy started to question me. But on the whole I've improved since I came here.'

'You've made one big mistake.'

'Several.'

'Only one that really matters. Life has its problems — but you've expected to solve them all. Why should there be a solution to everything? Probably Lieselotte Mölling solved one problem for you — for about as long as the solution was valid. You were lucky there; but in any case, you were out of your own mainstream. I don't think your Blanche brought you any solution at all, except in the first flush of finding each other, which isn't the best time for balanced perception. From what you've told me about her, she's in need of too many solutions herself. And your French girl-friend: she's the weakest straw you ever clutched at: little more than your own invention, in fact.'

'So where does my solution lie?'

'In not expecting to find one. Why should life owe you solutions? In my own case, it's easy. I am a creative artist. I synthesize my own illusions, and they satisfy me. I don't know whether you could do that. I don't know whether you have the talent.'

'But what can I do immediately?'

'Nothing. Just wait.'

CHAPTER 16

Kenworthy rang Wright's office from Liverpool Street, did not get Shiner, who was out in the field somewhere. He found his way to a sergeant who clearly knew his Inspector's mind and dispositions.

Kenworthy waxed skittishly wrathful: and breathless.

'Tell him that when it comes to jet-lag, there are bits of me catching up with myself all over Europe. Hook of Holland to Hamburg—a town on the North Sea coast that was like living under a wet Shetland blanket. And Everard's wartime lady-friend hasn't had a peep out of him for years. So all the way cross-country to Normandy—where Madame Besson hasn't heard a dicky-bird from Everard for months. He owes her answers to two letters, urgent ones, about one of his kid's billets that's had to go into quarantine. And so bus, train and night-flight to Innsbruck, then a toy train up the Zillertal. And Everard isn't in Hintertux, isn't in Hochbettleck, isn't in Brach, isn't in any bloody village that has a goat track leading into Hokey-Pokeyland. Only a bloody imbecile would be, at this time of year. Even Hannibal wouldn't have tackled it—unless he could have got hold of Dumbo.'

'I know that Inspector Wright is very anxious to contact you, sir.'

'Well, if he tries hard enough, I dare say he'll find me.'

Kenworthy went home for the rest of the day. Wright rang him in the middle of the afternoon.

'What the hell do you think you are on, Simon? There was a message waiting for me at the Yard—'

'Reporting failure of a mission. It was always on the cards, you know. For my money, Everard has pulled off his vanishing trick. I think he's still in this country.'

'Balls, ballocks, bullshit and bang-my-arse—and well you know it. Sealink have a record of his Dunkirk crossing on their passenger manifest. The Gare du Nord has a carbon copy of a seat reservation in his name. The Munich police have a registration: he spent the night at a hotel called the Stachus. And the Austrian police have accounted for him at a guesthouse near the Tirolean frontier where he's living under his own name, and the village constable is keeping an unobtrusive eye on him.'

The line went temporarily silent.

'All of which you obviously know for yourself. So what's the ploy, Simon?'

'Leave Everard alone. Time is doing its celebrated healing job. And let the British media think he's still constituting a menace around pubs, crystal-gazers and fruit machines. That will keep people on their mettle. Have you identified the girl on the beach yet?'

'Narrowing it down.'

'About time, too. See you, Shiner.'

'Just a minute—just a minute. Is that all you've got to tell me? Why can't some men retire properly while they're about it? I have to account for myself to others, you know.'

'Well, account for yourself, then. Good practice for you. You know very well that you've no real case on which you could pull Everard through the machine at the moment. If the time comes when you have—which it won't— you can get him out of Austria at the flick of a switch. He'd come voluntarily.'

Silence again, while Wright tried to digest all this.

'There's something I want to say to you, Simon— something that was on the tip of my tongue all those years when you were trying to teach me how not to be a detective: I bloody well hate you. When can we meet?'

Kenworthy went back to Warnford next morning, went at

once to buy another ounce of Mick M'Quaid from a tobacconist who not only remembered him, but was now convinced that he was officer in charge of the Everard-Shires case. He waited for another customer to go out, then bent under his counter for the latest, extraordinary edition of *The Collegian*:

Out of the Mouths of—

Two deaths: as unnecessary as they are tragic.

So where will Joseph Kite, alias William Townshend, alias—no; we must be careful—where will this middle-aged, respectable, paternalistic, obsessive traveller strike next?

Whom next will he persuade to appear in public with him in a green tam-o'-shanter? For make no mistake: Warnford's pathological killer is a great admirer of naïve femininity. He prefers his girls to look like girls.

Reminiscent, isn't that, of a phrase we have heard so often, whenever latter-day fashions have come under discussion in a certain tutorial room overlooking the Library Concourse? And which symbol of decency and light—we are not being satirical, we were very fond of Sue—which disingenuous child was it who was always most ready to leap to his support?

Yet we still find officialdom too timorous to press the Equals button at the bottom corner of their calculator. The Collegian *offers, therefore, without comment, a few more digits to be punched into the aggregate.*

Take Allouville, for example, an insignificant Norman village close to Yvetot, whose claim to glory is a twee little consecrated chapel, built into a hollow tree. What happened during last year's Easter holiday, when E and S crowded in there together? It is a dainty little chantry, which some might find emotionally overwhelming, and which affords barely room for two people. Were E and S emotionally overwhelmed in there? Ask

MG, or EBJ, or LFN—all of whom saw them come out.

Or let us come nearer home. What was E doing one filthy evening last February, as far from his home interests as Chert St Mary? Come to that, what was S doing there too? Further information from RT and EOW.

Finally, let us move nearer to events that we find, frankly, almost too terrible to contemplate. At ten minutes to eight one recent fatal morning (which of us can ever bear to travel on the 8.05 again?) E and S were seen in intense and fleeting conversation in a shop doorway in Warnford's new shopping precinct. At ten minutes to eight! Witness: JM. On a morning when, less than a quarter of an hour later, neither was to know that the other had entered a railway station and got on to a train! What other conclusion must E have drawn from the suitcase that S was carrying?

It would be, we feel sure, supererogatory to draw the attention of the town's (no, sorry—it is now the country's) leading sleuths to certain imponderables posed by the suitcase itself.

Kenworthy handed the paper back to the shopkeeper. 'And what's been the public reaction to this?'

'Monumental bad taste. And if these kids do know anything, they ought to be helping the police, not ribbing them. I don't know why Shepherd allows it.'

'You told me last time I was in that you know the Shires parents.'

'All my life. And they don't know what's hit them. They do not know.'

'Gen me up.'

The tobacconist stopped to think. Reactionary, intolerant observer of his fellow man, perpetually angry, discoverer of social decadence in most of what he saw, there was one subject on which he nevertheless wanted to be fair; and on which, though he knew his own mind, he had never had to express himself before in words that were going to influence another man's actions.

'Not swanky folk, you know. Live out in Rodings Street, which isn't exactly an estate agent's paradise. He's in accounts at Wetherby's, and his wife's just a Warnford girl, from before the time when light industry and commuters took the place over. Not churchy folk, not particularly— well, Easter and Christmas, you know— it's the girl who really got that bug. But decent folk, never owed a man a penny. And all they lived for was that girl.'

Kenworthy went to the Shires' home, one of Warnford's older terraces, a bay window with hyacinths in bowls in a room not much more than twelve feet by ten. The television set was a small portable black and white. The cleanliness was scrupulous, the decor appalling. It was hardly imaginable that such a consistent set of pictures could have been chosen without passing a qualifying course in mediocrity of taste: two assembly-line oil paintings of meadows with yellow willows; a proprietory calendar with a honeysuckled cottage whose metallic paint caught the light like the nap of a velvet; and over the mantelpiece an enormous wallpaper inset of Ullswater. There was a shelf of books that had been Susan's at an earlier age: an encyclopædia in bound weekly parts; Christmas annuals and a set of classics, still looking mint new in engine-tooled imitation leather. The parents' reading lay in two library books, left open over the arms of chairs: an R. F. Delderfield that had recently been run as a television serial, and a biography of second echelon royalty. They took the *Daily Mail* and one of the less glossy women's weeklies.

Henry Shires, still at home on a compassionate leave commutation, was facing manfully up to something that he neither understood nor yet fully believed. His wife controlled the sob that was still her reaction to any sympathetic stranger. They were the sort of couple to whom a daughter as potential primary teacher was scaling heights that they could never have considered within their own target area. And the emotional bludgeoning that they had undergone tended to come out in bursts of anger against matters that were only of marginal relevance. In this respect, the mother was more openly affected than the father.

'They've been so good at the school—the wreath that they sent! And nobody could have been sweeter than Dr Shepherd. But they never really appreciated her, you know. Her last school report: I shall never forgive them for that. As hard a worker as they ever had in that building—well, my husband can tell you what hours she put in at her books. And six O-levels! Yet there always had to be someone, at the end of every term, to spoil the picture.'

And Kenworthy had to look at those reports:

An industrious and skilled reproducer of received opinions. She now needs to evolve some of her own.

'How could we show that to her uncles and aunts?' her mother said. 'It makes it look as if she cheated in her work.'

If I have any criticism at all, it is of her over-readiness to believe everything that she is told. I wish she would argue with me sometimes.

'Well, what are teachers for, if they are not to be believed?'

'It isn't true, anyway,' her father said. 'She could argue the hind leg off a mule. That teacher ought to have heard her argue with *me*.'

'Ideas of her own, Mr Kenworthy? I used to say to her, I don't know where you get them from. She and her father at the Sunday dinner-table, it was like the Houses of Parliament. I used to say to them, oh, give it a rest, you two.'

'What sort of thing used she to argue about?'

'Everything under the sun—politics, religion, pop music—'

'Always in the nicest of spirits, you understand, never a raised voice.'

'She was a sweet-natured child.'

'When I say she argued about religion, I don't mean she disbelieved. You couldn't keep her away from church on Sundays. But she had—well, notions that I don't understand. Like the miracles. She said it didn't matter whether the miracles were true or not. It didn't make any difference to what the New Testament meant. I never could quite follow that, but I know she didn't mean it in any irreverent spirit.'

'And I used to say to her, if there's anything ever that worries you, there's your Bible in your bedroom. Open it, and your finger will light on something to comfort you.'

'What sort of pop music did she like?'

'Oh, what they all like. But she always gave way, if she wanted *Top of the Pops* and we wanted something else. She had her own little record player, up in her bedroom. And she liked the Bee Gees and Abba. And I'm afraid she liked the Beatles, too. But if ever one of us shouted up the stairs for her to turn the volume down, it was always done without a murmur.'

Kenworthy took them gently through the carrying of her suitcase to her interview, and the story did not vary from what they had told to Shiner.

'Last year, one of her friends had gone up for interview, just the same as she did, and was asked to stay the night, and she said she wasn't going to be caught out if it happened to her. And how she hoped it would be so! I could tell.'

There was no mention, no suspicion, it seemed, of *Jesus Christ Superstar*. Kenworthy came at it obliquely.

'Did she often go up to London?'

'Quite often. She and some of her friends always used to have a shopping spree in Oxford Street at the beginning of the Christmas holidays—had done ever since she was about thirteen. Then there was something always going on from the college: trips to see paintings, the Royal Festival Hall—'

'Was this the first time she had been up to town on her own?'

'I suppose it was, when you come to think about it.'

'Did she ever want to go to things that you and your husband weren't keen on?'

'She was not a wilful girl at all, Mr Kenworthy. She might have argued with her Dad, but she'd never have gone against us.'

'I'm sure, Mrs Shires. I was thinking of things that young people often don't see eye to eye about. Like pop music. I think there are more family differences on that score—'

'Oh—no, no, no—there was never anything like that. We never had *differences*. Like these open-air pop concerts they have—they always disgusted her.'

'I was thinking rather of musicals—things like *Godspell*—'

'She did go to that, with the church. But *Jesus Christ Superstar*—that was the one that she never did get to. When they went from the college, she was down with the flu. And when the church youth club got up a party, she was tied up with a play—painting scenery. She always said she felt doomed not to see *Jesus Christ Superstar*.'

'Who were her friends?'

'Oh, she had nice friends. Girls like herself: Brenda Thwaites, Lucy Turner, Mary Gallon. She never went about with the wild bunch.'

'Boy-friends?'

'Nothing serious, you know. She'd go to dances at the Church Hall and the college. And there's a boy in the next road who used to take her to the cinema sometimes. But he's gone to Southampton University, and he didn't seem interested in her, this last holiday.'

As Kenworthy was making ready to go, Mr Shires showed that he had one further thought on his mind.

'There's something we'd both like to say, Mr Kenworthy: this teacher, Mr Everard. Nobody will ever make us believe that he had anything to do with what happened. She was very fond of him and he was fond of her. And I don't know what can have come over him, going off the way that he has. But that's a coincidence. It is not on the cards, Mr Kenworthy, that that man could have laid a finger on her. Susan always used to say it was horrible, the way some of them used to get on to him, up at the college. And many a time she has spoken up in his defence. So much for not having ideas of her own. Her mother and I met him several times, at teachers' at-homes. And we used to say, there sits a gentleman.'

'I'm sure you are right,' Kenworthy told them.

CHAPTER 17

There came an evening when Everard looked at Hilde Kornahl in a certain way. They were alone in the bar and the waitress had brought a candle to their table as if she were intent on stage-managing the setting. Everard had shifted his taste to Hilde's light white wine and had bought half a bottle, from which she had said she would only take one glass. The light played on her cheeks and hair and he looked at her with a frankness that she could hardly misinterpret. What is more, Hilde Kornahl, who must surely be aware of what he was trying to radiate, gave no sign of deflecting it. He felt, or imagined he felt, a reciprocal message.

They talked: about the astounding lack of future promise in the pages of the early Rilke. But there was nothing impassioned in the literary views of either of them. Conversation was a whiling-away of the sluggish wake of a dilatory clock. He finished his second glass of wine rather quickly.

'You could have saved that for tomorrow,' she said.

'There are times when a man wants everything today.'

She leaned back and away, the better to study him over the table.

'There are times when I have thought you a strange man—a nice strange man. Now are you being merely a man.'

'A *nice* strange man?'

She shook her head enigmatically.

'It can spoil things between people if they know each too well. There ought to remain an element of mystery.'

A few minutes later, she said she was ready for early bed. He said that he was, too. When they were both on their feet, and he was moving a chair to let her away from the table, she put a hand on his wrist. He was surprised by the coolness of her flesh; and by its effect on him.

'This won't be a solution,' she said. 'But it will be nice.'

He went stealthily to her room. She had still not begun to undress. She went into her bathroom and insisted on darkness before she came back to him. Her bed was larger than his, a warm nest of duvet. His impression of her room was of the extra space and luxury that befitted a permanent resident, as against himself as a passing lodger.

Her perfume was vertiginous. There had to be an adjustment of bodies and limbs that did not know their way about each other; they achieved it. Lieselotte had sometimes seemed to want to consume him. Blanche could never escape from her own inflexibility. Hilde Kornahl applied herself to him; even in their intimacy, he wondered how consciously—how conscientiously. He had one fear—of being precipitous; in the outcome, it was neither one thing nor the other. He was awake for a long time afterwards; she appeared to be sleeping in untroubled calm.

The Zum Weissen Bock was awake and at work when he eventually walked back to his room along the chilly corridors, but as far as he was aware he was observed by no one. Hilde Kornahl had her breakfast sent up to her room and he did not see her again till midday, when she took a ten-minute walk to the end of the reservoir. He went out and joined her and was struck afresh by her grace, her wealth (she was wearing furs that must have been worth two or three years of his salary) and by those porcelain cheeks.

She teased him at first, gently, talking about things that could interest neither of them. Only when they turned at the muffled and distant sound of the lunch-gong did she relieve his suspense.

'You gave me something to remember, too—but we shall not make a habit of it. I have to be thrifty with my emotional reserves.'

He did not know what she meant, but when they reached the gateway of the guesthouse, she gripped his hand. 'Promise me you'll never try to find out—but one day you may discover how old I am.'

CHAPTER 18

'Just a pack of bored and thoughtless fools,' Leyton said. 'Wright asked me to clear it for him, and with a sergeant and two men I spent a three-session day on that issue of *The Collegian*. None of it helps us.'

It was to talk about that that Kenworthy had come again to his office.

'Item one: chapel in a hollow tree in Normandy. That exists. It's one of the sights in a round trip that Everard used to make with his pupils to Fécamp and Etretat. Witnesses: Mary Gallon, Eric Johnson and Linda Norris. They all saw Everard and Susan Shires come out of that tree together. It was a tight squeeze, and made comic because each was trying to give precedence to the other. More than comic: there was an accidental instant when they were in very close and suggestive contact. Girlish laughter. End of incident.'

The Warnford inspector straightened the edge of a sheet of paper in one of his filing baskets.

'Item two, not worth the weight of its own ink. What was E doing, one evening in February, as far from his home as the village of Chert St Mary? Second question: what was S also doing there? Witnesses; Robert Thomson and Eileen Worrall. Answers, one: Everard had been lecturing the Parent-Teacher Association of the Primary School on getting the most out of a family holiday abroad; two: Susan Shires had been delivering a birthday present to an aunt who lives in Chert. The pair of them met and waited together in the drizzle at the bus stop. They chatted. They sat together on the bus and chatted further. The pair who saw them knew bloody well that there was nothing in it. But Susan was being teased a lot because it was rumoured that she had a crush on Everard; and it seems pretty clear that they were playing her up because they could see she was sensitive to it. So it became a stupid talking point the next day—and kept alive for several days afterwards. Disposal of item.'

'How keen were these witnesses to answer your questions?'

'Nice kids, most of them. They said at once that there was nothing in what had been printed. But of course, I still had to put them through the works to make sure of it.'

'They hadn't collaborated in writing the article?'

'No. That was pure Fairbrother. They'd been surprised — and very annoyed — to have their initials quoted. Mary Gallon, particularly, was a close friend of Susan's, and has been going through a bad time since the murder.'

'And item three?'

'That also took us a long time. It was Judith Martin who saw Everard and Susan talking in a doorway in the Shopping Precinct, a quarter of an hour before the departure of their train. I took her up hill and down dale, several times over and inside out, through details that she couldn't have known if it hadn't been true. What Susan was wearing, and so forth.'

'A green tam-o'-shanter?'

'And the rest, Mr Kenworthy. We're not mugs, you know, even out here in the wilds.'

'And Judith Martin is Fairbrother's girl-friend?'

'Correct.'

'And what was she doing herself, about town at that hour of the morning? She struck me as the type who would stick to her bed till the last feasible minute — including flexitime.'

'We thought of that, too, we Warnford rustics. The previous evening she had been down to a girl-friend's, Liz Seymour, to compare notes for an essay that they were writing on a French playwright. Half a minute: Anouilh — is that how you pronounce it? We'd better get things bang to rights on all this. She'd left her notes behind and needed them for first lesson that morning. So she set her alarm and went down to fetch them.'

'Isn't Liz Seymour on the phone?'

'No.'

'But does she confirm about the notes?'

'Yes — but uncomfortably, I thought. I think she's lying.'

'We're up against a set of clever young buggers,' Kenworthy said. 'Are they doing it just for the sake of aggro and anarchy, do you think?'

'It would figure. It's the way Fairbrother has behaved ever since he set foot in the college.'

'You've had a word with Shepherd about him?'

'For what that was worth. He's on Fairbrother's side, of course, says that the lad is a bundle of nerves, under the extrovert pose. But he has a brilliant future, when he grows out of his facetiousness.'

'I am going to talk to Mary Gallon.'

Susan's friend had been kept home from the college that day, in a state of near prostration after having been put through the hoop over the *Collegian* article. Her home was not dissimilar to Susan's, and she and Susan had been in the same class since they were five years old.

Kenworthy did not even mention the tree-chapel incident, which had been her only connection with the article. But he asked her whether Susan had ever been to see *Jesus Christ Superstar*.

'It's funny you should ask that. Twice she should have gone, and twice she couldn't at the last moment. She said she was fated never to see it.'

'And didn't she make any plan to go later?'

'Vaguely. We thought we might go together next holiday. Susan said it would be just her luck for it to be taken off.'

'She hadn't said anything more precise about going?'

'No. Why should she? Why are you asking these questions?'

Mary Gallon was mildly sedated, and her mother was hovering.

'No reason at all, Mary. And I'd like it best if you didn't tell anyone what I've been asking. It just looks as if someone has been starting up another silly old rumour.'

His calls in Warnford were completed by lunch-time, and

Kenworthy was crossing London with a healthy portion of afternoon still in front of him. Having established that Wright would be in his office, he stopped off at New Scotland Yard on his way to Victoria.

Wright was just about to set out on another mortuary visit. The mortuary, he said, was becoming almost as immutable a feature in his life as poached egg on toast for his canteen snack. There had been, literally, a queue to see the body. On one occasion he had seen three consecutive visitors through without himself leaving the premises. They had come, distressed mothers, manly fathers and conscience-stricken elder sisters, in trepidation nourished by hours of build-up, wondering if they could bear to look on the features of the once loved and now mutilated dead. From Blackpool, Leeds, Lanchester in County Durham and Amesbury on Salisbury Plain: shaking their heads in distressed disclaimer, solemnly apologizing for not being related to the waxen face that lay against clinically cold white linen, amid hair disentangled and drawn tight by a conscientious and uninvolved mortician. Suffocation inside a plastic bag, at the foot of a sand path signposted *Beach*, does not leave the human face immediately recognizable, except to the intimate. The photographs had been too horrible and too unreliable to serve more than specialized viewers.

But now one of the recipients, an Inspector Pocock, functioning among the green fields of Hertfordshire, had rung through personally.

'I have a woman here who says she's absolutely certain: a social worker who specializes in the resettlement of the mentally disturbed. Shall I send her over to you? She's perfectly capable of organizing her own transport.'

Sal Comber looked at first sight more like one of her own resettlement cases, and not one for whom it would be easy to find a billet, a job, or even her just DHSS entitlements.

She was wearing denim slacks, thread-worn over her shoes and a patchwork jacket held loosely with wooden toggles. But on closer inspection she was nearer thirty-five than the twenty-two that she first appeared. She was brisk: to the extent of distrust and contempt for the police — which she assumed in advance that they expected. She was not impressed, as mere amateurs had been, by the unhushed official procedures of the mortuary, its refrigerated lockers and its tea-drinking attendant. But she was shaken by the sight of the corpse: more visibly affected than the matron from Blackpool or the young divorcee from Amesbury. But then, she was the only one in the long succession who had actually known the girl.

'Yes. That's Peggy Bentham. I told her she should have held on.'

Penny Bentham had been seventeen. When she was seven, her father had been given a life sentence for the murder of her mother and two of her siblings. There were some who said that the mother had deserved all that had come to her; the siblings had simply happened to be on hand at the moment of high passion. So, for that matter, had Penny, who had witnessed all three murders — and a kitchen cleaver is not the prettiest of instruments with which to see a domestic difference settled. Penny was the eldest, had picked up empirically some rough and ready short-cuts to survival, and had escaped almost naked to a neighbour; who for agonizing minutes had refused to admit her.

Wright and Kenworthy together took Sal Comber to a restaurant where they could be certain of a screened and respected corner, more conducive to illusions of confidentiality than an office with HMSO furniture. The social worker recovered quickly from her shock; but sobering traces of it remained, and showed themselves in a rather less abrasive attitude to the fuzz.

'I suppose it had to come sooner or later. You can work

your fingers to the bone fobbing something off, and five hundred hours of grafting can be wiped out in a single second.'

Sal Comber's trouble was that she assumed naturally that Welfare and the Old Bill were pulling in opposite directions. Both Kenworthy and Wright were too experienced to make any effort to persuade her, though every other sentence was an invitation to try.

They learned that Penny Bentham had been taken into care, at first into a small foster family where she developed — or assumed — autistic symptoms. That was as far as concerned the foster-parents, schoolteachers and visiting officials. None of these could establish any kind of communication with her. But she lacked neither the means nor the will to express herself with the younger occupants of the foster hearth, all of whom were wrestling with problems of their own. Penny Bentham was a reagent, releasing latent venoms and explosive gases. She had to be moved on; to a smaller home — and then to a larger one; to an institution; to a remand centre when magistrates called for reports on a shoplifting charge. She was given probation, broke it; was given extended probation, left school, was found a job that was an act of faith on the part of everyone who had a hand in the gerrymandering of it.

She did astonishingly well there; it was a small office, handling the six employees and regular contracts of a light-engineering sub-contractor. No one ever understood why, at the height of apparent success, she walked out on them without notice. She was found drunk almost to the point of alcoholic poisoning under the hoar-frost of a layby, having been picked up and put down again by an unidentified lorry driver. Or a van driver. Or an executive Jag.

There had been no sexual interference. In the state she was in, she could have appealed only to a necrophile. But then, it stood out through her record, even in the depths of her recidivism, her determination to keep herself sexually to herself. That, too, was derived from observations made before the age of seven.

She was referred for psychiatric report and was detained for observation for the statutory twenty-eight days. As she was not charged with an offence for which she could be imprisoned, the court had no powers to make a compulsory hospital order, and she was duly released back into the care of the Local Authority. In court, shaky from prolonged sedation, but cleaned up and cosmeticized by a nurse with five minutes to spare, she was a figure for whom outside observers could harbour some hope: politely spoken, almost demure, with a touch of the fey in her modestly lowered eyes. Penny Bentham had some of the makings of an actress.

She now became expert on her entitlements at the Ministry of Social Security, got to know her way round the regulations better than some of the clerks who tried to frustrate her, was picked up on the outskirts of a Class C drug case, in which the Poor Man's Lawyer unsuccessfully submitted that the evidence was planted. This time she found herself compulsorily detained in the same hospital she had visited before.

Labels are convenient in any branch of medicine; Penny Bentham became a chartered psychopath. She learned a great deal about manipulating to her advantage the mightily important trivialities of ward life; and when she kicked over the traces was awarded solitary confinement, electric shock treatment and quasi-punitive sedation. Three times she cut loose, once for a prolonged period, of which the details remained known only to herself. She eventually surrendered, at the house of a hospitable policeman, after a cold night alfresco. The period of liberty that culminated on a sandy beach was her fourth.

'I told her to hold on,' Sal Comber repeated. 'We'd

reached the stage where I'd been called into the hospital to renew our acquaintance. There seemed every chance that in a month or two we'd be able to try her outside again, take the pitcher back to the well. Then one particular nurse went on leave. It wouldn't be true to say the only nurse who ever showed Penny any kindness; the only one from whom Penny seemed prepared to accept it. Now for a fortnight she had to make do with substitutes, nurses who knew her less intimately, had less time and less patience, who didn't appreciate the territorial rights she'd carved out for herself in the hospital.'

'One nurse?' Kenworthy said. 'A *male* nurse?'

They saw him in a stockroom that the Administrative Secretary put at their disposal: George Lamplugh, a man in a white coat, with an almost bald head and eyebrows that darted remarkably upwards at their outer corners. He was a solemn man, who thought before he answered pertinent questions; and had a balanced view of the prospects and limitations — the ultimate impossibilities, in fact — of his job.

'Of course, the trouble is, in this country we don't analyse. The forces are spread out too thinly. We sedate. We opt for the easier life. And I suggest that if you gentlemen were to try a forty-eight hour stint in here, you'd vote the same way. Penny, now: there was a case crying out for analysis.'

'One moment,' Kenworthy asked. 'Where did you actually spend your leave?'

'In a caravan lent by a friend, on the Pembroke coast.'

'Alone? In November?'

'Snug and warm: Calor gas. And a chance to catch up on my reading. An opportunity *not* to meet people. I can give you the name and address of the local keyholder.'

'I'm sure you can. Do you mind, Inspector Wright, if I ask a few more questions?'

Kenworthy treated Wright almost farcically formally in front of some kinds of public. He had insisted on refreshing himself from the main file, had sat reading throughout the preliminaries.

'You say that the waiting list is too long for analysis. I don't doubt it. But a good nurse could do as much as some of the doctors, couldn't he, given time, place and scope? You could have put Penny Bentham on her feet, couldn't you—if only you could have her to yourself for long enough, without fear of interference? Including a timely injection of sex: not a therapy to be ignored—especially in the case of a girl who needed to adjust her ideas to it. A lot of men have a boundless belief in sex as a therapy. It isn't always shared without qualification by their womenfolk.'

'I don't know what you're talking about.'

'I'll lay it on the line, then. You spent two days of your leave in Wales, enough to establish that you were there. Then you came back and got Penny Bentham out; whether with or without her previous knowledge and connivance doesn't bother me for the moment. You hired a car; perhaps you'd already got that for the Pembroke jaunt. You went up the east coast. And once you got her out in the big wide world, you found Peggy Bentham not as easy to handle as you'd thought she was going to be. She was a friendly lass in the hospital—when she was jockeying for privileges. But now she could be moody and unpredictable, up one minute, down the next. And she could be quite careless about the dangers of your position, couldn't she? Do you remember that stationer's shop, where you bought a map and she tried to buy a comic birthday card to send to somebody back in the ward? You took that off her, didn't you? Then she insisted on all that stupidity with Gypsy Rosanna. Doesn't that show how pathetic her basic insecurity was?'

Wright was sitting back, not quite smiling.

'At the Coastguard you had one stroke of good luck and one of bad. Gladys Turnbull thought she knew who you were. Did she actually tell you so, by the way, on the side, promising you you had nothing to fear from her? You tried to have sex with Penny that night, but she still wouldn't have it. Who knows why? All part of being a psychopath, I suppose. And you must have been getting desperate for it. She left you, while you were asleep, went out on the sand dunes at midnight, acting, ballet-dancing, back where she was in the worst of her disorder. You woke, missed her, went and fetched her back. She didn't want to come at first. One of the fishermen told us. Yours was the oddest of love-hate relationships, wasn't it, oscillating almost by the minute? And then she was suddenly back on your shoulder; a reaction to the beauty of the night perhaps. You certainly had taken something on, hadn't you?'

Lamplugh's strange eyebrows jutted up like mitred edges. There were points that he wanted to answer, but Kenworthy would allow no interruption.

'You seduced her. I don't know how—but it's been done before. And then you knew that you were in trouble. Did you actually hear Mrs Turnbull stop and listen on the landing? Perhaps not. But you left other evidence behind that wasn't easily got rid of, didn't you? There's a cold light of dawn after some moments of ecstasy, isn't there? A state registered mental nurse, having intercourse with a patient, whom he knows to be under treatment for a mental disorder; what does the Sexual Offences Act of 1956 have to say about that? But you knew about the Everard-Shires case now inspiring the newspapers. Why not have this incident firmly put down to Everard? You left an envelope with his name on it, just to clinch matters. But then you made a horribly stupid mistake. You should never have gone on to Hunstanton. You ought to have got right out of East Anglia. I can't think what got into you—unless, of course, the girl was now such a handful that you were driven distracted. I honestly believe that you thought at first that you could help her, Lamplugh. But you're not a doctor; and girls like Penny Bentham need the full resources of a hospital. You went to a chemist's and tried to get specialized sedatives. What were you after: largactil? You got hold of every newspaper you could, mugged up every available detail about Susan Shires. You even bought Penny new clothes, told her you liked her to look like a girl. What really mattered was getting hold of a green tam-o'-shanter. You were lucky at the Braemar in that Penny kept to her room. As long as you did not appear in public with her, nobody knew who the hell you were. Then a man approached you in a pub, and you knew you had fallen into your own trap.'

'Pure fantasy. That's all this is.'

'Let me at least finish it. The next morning, Penny was in more amenable mood. You told her this man was on your heels, and the business of giving him the slip appealed to her sense of intrigue. That's why she turned round and grinned at him. You got away. All you needed now was a quiet beach. And you're a strong man, Lamplugh. Male nurses need to be. All right Inspector—I think you can start doing your stuff now.'

Wright stirred himself into life, but looked not altogether certain.

'I guarantee you'll have defence-proof evidence,' Kenworthy said.

So Lamplugh was cautioned and taken away to be helpful. It was late the next morning before Kenworthy came back—with a miscellaneous cargo.

An identification parade, mounted scrupulously according to the book, was held in the police station yard. Rosie-Anne, her hair ludicrously piled, her coat bizarrely shabby, looked at the line of men without assurance, walked past Lamplugh three times without recognizing him, then shook her head.

Lamplugh bore a look of smug pleasure, but the parade was told to stand firm. Gladys Turnbull was then brought in, her tears ruining her mascara. But she had strong views about the sort of deception that had been practised on her, and no inhibition about indicating Lamplugh. She was followed by two beach fishermen, exiled without compassion from a propitious tide. They wasted as little time as possible in picking out their quarry.

Finally, the station inspector brought in a greasy-haired man wearing the tie of some poor man's school, club or regiment. Lamplugh snarled at the sight of him, and had to be held back from actual physical attack. Two hours later, his statement was well advanced.

'Very neat, Shiner,' Kenworthy said. 'But I fear it's the second half of this case that's going to need ingenuity.'

CHAPTER 19

Everard's motives were — and remain — obscure. His walk into the night was not, perhaps, suicidal in intent. It hardly fell within the proverbial 'call for help' category, since he had taken no steps, even of a devious nature, to ensure that any help was available. Nor could he have had any intelligent hope of ever reaching Italy, or for that matter of getting more than a quarter of a mile out of Brach. Perhaps there was a touch of Russian roulette about it; perhaps he wanted to give his guardian spirits a chance to show their hand.

He went out for a walk from the Gasthof after dinner, having drunk two warming *Havelschnapps* with his coffee. He wrapped up well, muffled his throat against the icy wind that would work havoc with his respiratory blood vessels, slipped a trinitrate tablet under his tongue and began up the hill.

The snow had been cleared in the immediate vicinity of the guesthouse and the going was easy. But he had not made fifty yards before it was borne in on him that the tablet was not going to work. It happened sometimes. The drug deteriorated, however careful one might be about protecting it from sunlight and changes of temperature. The familiar pain gripped his chest, immobilized his left arm, drew up his fingers, stabbed him in the larynx. He ought to have noticed the bubble on the pill; he wondered how many he had left that could still be relied on.

He stood still for the pain to subside, which it did, slowly, his circulation struggling to reassert itself against the cold. When he felt recovered, he went on again, but was forced to a standstill after not more than twelve paces. What he needed was another pill. It was a situation that he had been in before, when the effort of getting off his gloves, of fumbling for the bottle, of unscrewing its cap, seemed too great to be faced. He went another six paces, and the pain returned.

So should he go back to Zum Weissen Bock? Even the downhill distance seemed forbidding. He turned to put the wind behind him. Pulled off one glove, dropped it in the snow, knew that to stoop for it would bring on an intolerable spasm. He got at the phial, his fingers already freezing, tried to see by the moonlight on the palm of his hand which pills were still unaffected by the ruinous bubble, managed to scatter two thirds of them about the ice at his feet. He took one, felt the burning saliva that showed that it was effective. But he had left it so late that it made him want to vomit. He bent for the glove, slipped and fell, felt the snow, melted by the heat of his body, soaking in through his greatcoat.

'Telephone for Herr Everard.'

The landlord looked to Fräulein Kornahl for intellectual help in a crisis. She took the receiver.

'Ja, Herr Kenworthy—we'll have to get him to ring back. Where is he?'

'Out,' the landlord said.

'Good God! No: let me go and get him. I know which way he'll have gone.'

CHAPTER 20

The Copa Cabana had become noticeably less popular since the death of Susan Shires had become known. Justin Fairbrother's group had now shrunk to four, of whom Judith Martin was now the only girl. Justin too had evidently been affected by the pathos of the human condition, for he had developed a facial tic, besides the occasional twitching of his shoulders. But he put on a display when Kenworthy came in.

'Ah! Consoling to know that we have not been abandoned.'

Kenworthy nodded courteously to him, as he might have done to the Yard's commissioner if he had met him in mufti at the seaside. He included Judith Martin in his greeting. She merely raised reptilian eyes to his for the briefest instant, assuring him of the most consummate hatred that one human could muster for another. Kenworthy had made unobtrusive enquiries about her in the town. Her father was a second-hand car dealer, but she was the sort of daughter that any man in the present state of society could have: tastes outlandish to any generation but her own, professedly anarchical in politics, ethics and religion, yet content to receive an unearned allowance, and indeed constantly managing to have it indexed to her ever-expanding tastes.

The group were passing round a piece of paper when Kenworthy arrived. A boy whose name he did not know was on the point of handing it to Judith. Kenworthy promptly intercepted it and carried it with him to the serving counter.

'You have no right whatever to do that.'

'I have no rights whatever. Except, in certain circumstances which it is always risky to exploit, the right of citizen's arrest.'

Justin stood up, squared up to him, looked for a moment as if he were prepared to fight for the document. Kenworthy folded it without reading it, put it away in an inside pocket. If there were going to be a fight, it would now be a fundamental one.

'It means nothing, anyway.'

Justin sat down. Kenworthy ordered a coffee and examined the cakes on a glass shelf.

'I'll have a chocolate biscuit, please. At least that's wrapped in foil.'

The black-haired woman who ran the place looked at him with unspoken poison. He sat for a while in self-composing silence before taking the paper out. And the silence affected Fairbrother's quartet too. There were no voices loud with anarchical banter now.

Kenworthy unfolded the paper. It was a sheet torn from a student's economy pad, and though its contents were only in note form, they were written in Fairbrother's stylish Chancery hand. It seemed to be a skeleton draft for the next *Collegian* leader.

Where Old Bill Fears to Tread . . .

Intr: Big guns deployed; comings and goings; midnight oil; prestigious figure from Gold Past called in to watch interests of E's wife.

Trust authorities grateful to Collegian *for previous leads; refer (mock heroics) to man-hours spent investigating hollow tree in Allouville. Refer bullying inno-*

cent parties; MG absent school on verge breakdown.

Collegian now offers further revelations from own London Correspo.ident. Refer old boy network in colleges, City, etc.

Parenthesis: long arm coincidence; how many classic crimes finally solved thanks lucky stroke?

E and S seen together in London, mid-evening operative day. (Query: witnesses? Two from KH, JR, TB, NF; check.) Not really staggering coincidence: large number flock Victoria Stn. E and S in pub (S under age, but refer graciously to temperance habits).

Query: Conversation overheard? Suspicious behaviour? S high.

'Dangerous stuff,' Kenworthy said across the room. 'You disappoint me, Fairbrother. I'll try to continue to admire your intelligence. I'll try to make myself believe that you'd never have used this. And do you think any of your witnesses would have played ball? Though I suppose that one or more of them may be as deeply up to the neck in it as you are.'

'That's a private document,' Fairbrother said. 'We were looking at purely fictitious possibilities — hypotheses — a scenario. Isn't that the way you go to work sometimes?'

'Pitiful, Fairbrother. You'll have to try harder than that. You've overreached yourself this time.'

'There are two or three dozen meanings that could be attached to what's on that piece of paper.'

'Really? I can see only one.'

Kenworthy got up and moved his coffee to another table, from which he could command the group.

'Did you ever go to see *Jesus Christ Superstar?*' he asked, with one of his enigmatic changes of tone.

'I don't see what —'

'I'm asking you a very simple question. Let me break it down a stage further. I know that a party to see the show

was once got up in your college. I just want to know
whether you were a member of that party.'

Fairbrother looked at him as if he doubted his mental
stability.

'Well—I am asking you: were you, or weren't you?'

'As a matter of fact I was. But that was a year ago—'

Kenworthy turned to Judith Martin.

'Did you go too?'

'No way. Not my scene.'

'Really? I would have thought that the outing mattered
more than the play itself.'

'As a matter of fact, there was a flu epidemic at the
time. I couldn't go.'

She looked at him with the skin stretched tight across
her browless forehead, her eyes insolently sluggish.

'You weren't the only one in that position, were you?
Well, now I'm going to do a dangerous thing. I'm going
to exercise my imagination. And shall I tell you why I call
it a dangerous thing? I'm going to make up what you
might call a hypothetical scenario. I'm basing it on prob-
abilities: on my knowledge of certain facts and personalities. I am bound to make some mistakes, because
there are some essentials that I cannot possibly know.
And when I do trip up here and there, you are going to
feel frightfully superior. You're going to have the advantage of me, and think I'm a bumbling old fool who can't
get my facts right. See what I mean?'

His manner was sweetly reasonable and he was speaking as pleasantly to them as if they were small and biddable children with whom he was pleading for a code of
nursery conduct.

'Listen with Kenworthy, then. Are you sitting comfortably? Right; I'll begin.'

He looked at each of their faces in turn, including the
unnamed couple who had not spoken, and were sitting in
embarrassment, not looking at anyone.

'One morning earlier this term, Susan Shires received a letter inviting her to an interview at a London training college. She was understandably excited about it, and started telling people as soon as she arrived on your campus—is that what you call it? And of course news about interviews, academic careers, is of universal interest, because you're all at some stage or other of the same game. So even people who aren't normally friends take an interest. Like you, Judith Martin—well: Susan is talking to you, and you are sharing her pleasure. I suppose that even you are capable of being nice to someone some of the time. And you say, "Lucky old you," or words conveying that meaning. "A day off, and a day in London at that. What are you going to do with yourself: come straight home again?" And she says she hasn't made up her mind yet, but she'd love to see *Jesus Christ Superstar*. And you, on an impulse, say, "I missed it, too. I'll come with you. I'll come up after afternoon school." And you give her the name of a grotty hotel, where she can go and book beds for you, because there are all sorts of former college students about town, and you'll probably get some sort of party going after the show. Am I roughly on the right lines?'

No one answered him, so he went straight on, cheerfully.

'I don't know whether you went to the theatre or not. I don't particularly care, because it isn't all that relevant. I am sure that there was some sort of party, attended among others by some whose initials you were going to quote in your next batch of witnesses. I do know that something happened at that party, including the foul prank of lacing food or drink for Susan Shires with LSD-25—one of the few drugs that you can feed to a victim without her knowledge. Another characteristic of the same drug is that no one knows in advance how any particular subject is going to react to it. There are hoary and probably apocryphal old stories of hallucinations with super-confidence, so that people try flying out of fifth-storey windows, and jumping down stairwells. Do tell me, by the way, am I veering horribly off course?'

No one wished to navigate for him. He continued.

'Nasty though all this is, you have had certain things, as they say nowadays, going for you. Susan Shires isn't going to give evidence; and that poor devil Everard has gone walkabout. So you start your poison campaign. It isn't even all that important what sort of issues you throw up. They may seem relatively trivial in that ghastly news-sheet of yours, but they're doing their job, keeping people's minds on a certain possibility. I personally think you would have been extremely ill-advised to try to throw up a London angle too. But maybe you'd have had second thoughts and not printed it. And sooner or later, with any luck, the news is going to come in that something has happened to Everard. He's known to have a dangerous heart condition, and the chances are that he's adopted a lifestyle that's going to hasten things. He'll either never show up again—fleeing from his own guilt?—or he'll just die. Perhaps then the Susan Shires file will be closed altogether. There's no proof that Everard was the murderer, but the more pointers you can strew about, the greater your hope that the Susan Shires case will be allowed to gather dust in a corner. I hope you're still with me?'

Justin Fairbrother had now assumed an attempt at a superior smirk. His girl-friend was now looking at a spot on the floor some eight feet away from her.

'Well: I have one piece of news for you. And I trust that however well it may fit in with your best-laid plans, it might just have some shade of other meaning for you. John Everard is dead. He set out for a nocturnal walk on the flank of an Austrian mountain—a pilgrimage that I don't think he even hoped to complete. He was a popular man in his guesthouse—much more so than ever he was in your college—and a rescue party was hard on his heels.

But they were too late. So there you are. Not, I fear, that
it is going to help you now.'

A flush had come into Fairbrother's cheeks. One of the
nonentities swallowed; and Judith sighed, as if with
boredom.

And then the street door opened, all eyes were switched
to it, and the little café seemed suddenly to be full of
vigorous limbs: Inspector Leyton with one of his sergeants
and Inspector Wright with one of his; also a couple of
uniformed constables and a policewoman.

'Do come in, my friends. I was just explaining to these
young people how we come to know all about them. Shall
I go on?'

Judith Martin stood up.

'This is absurd! And you're going to make us miss
another history tutorial.'

'Sit down!'

And the men in uniform deployed themselves signifi-
cantly.

'I would like to continue. I think you must agree that
we haven't quite completed the picture yet. It's puzzled
me a little ever since I started thinking about this, why
you should have bothered to puncture the integrity of
Susan Shires. Such a mouse: I was tempted to think that
she might be beneath you—so colourlessly compliant, so
incapable of making anything of herself—even if she ever
were to kick over the traces. But of course, there was
another side to Susan. She wasn't as complacent about
the state of her life as all that. She honoured her father
and mother, as the old law demanded. But that isn't to
say that she didn't sometimes resent the relentless pro-
saicness. She had a home in which she couldn't really talk
ideas at all. She could never even properly discuss the
work she was doing in college. The way she approached
her visit to *Jesus Christ Superstar* was pure deceit, planned in
advance: because she was fed up to the back teeth with

opposition to her doing things. Let her mention going to a London theatre alone, and there'd have been another argument, another fight with frustration. The yarn about the chance of a night in a guest room at training college was much more trouble-free. And maybe her parents would have objected too to the company she was keeping, if they'd known she was meeting you two. I know I would have done, if I'd been her father. But never mind that. What I am saying is that Susan Shires, bless her heart, was—quite exceptionally for her—in mid-rebellion of a sort when she met you two that evening. And that helped to put ideas into your head: let's see how far old Sue will go.

'I'm sorry if I'm monopolizing this conversation. And as I said at the beginning, I'm probably getting quite a lot of my facts wrong. Does either of you want to add anything at this stage?'

But even if either of them had had a mind to speak, the next interruption would have obstructed it. The door opened again, and this time it was a man in a new dark overcoat, with the slightly dazed expression of a shepherded convalescent. John Everard: he held the door for his wife to precede him; very primly, and looking at Justin and Judith with tightened lips.

'I think you have met everyone here—especially those two in the middle there—'

Fairbrother was visibly shocked. The appearance of Everard made no real difference to the logic of events, but it was a jolt. The youth half opened his mouth to say something, then closed it again. He looked as if he were about to stand up from his chair, then had second thoughts about that, too. For the first time, there was fear in the girl's eyes.

Kenworthy smiled at them.

'You see—my imagination leads me forever astray. I must have got it all wrong about that walk up the Gänse-

joch. The rescue party must have been in time after all.
So I am afraid the file is not going to be put away on that
account. And now, as I am a man completely without official standing, with no wish at all to steal thunderbolts
from the gods, I will withdraw from the fray. Except—'

He paused, pure and unashamed ham acting.

'My sense of poetry calls for some sort of coda: or
should the word be envoi? Do you mind, Inspector
Wright, if I ask half a dozen more questions?'

Shiner played the part of foil to him and Kenworthy
got up and went and stood facing Judith.

'I hate to bore you, and I know that you've gone over all
this before. But I would like to satisfy myself on one
point. Just tell me what Susan Shires was wearing when
you saw her talking to Mr Everard in a doorway in the
shopping precinct, a quarter of an hour before their train
went.'

For seconds it looked as if she were going to refuse to
say a word. Kenworthy repeated the request, very slowly,
in exactly the same words, but in a tone that he had not
previously used this morning.

She began to answer in a voice so weak that there was a
strained silence, everyone in the room trying to catch
what she said.

When she had finished, Kenworthy turned to Leyton.

'That's consistent with what she told you?'

'It is.'

'Inspector Wright—are those the clothes that were
found on the body?'

'Yes, Mr Kenworthy.'

'Good. Though not all that clever, perhaps, since she
would have been wearing them at the party at which she
died. Now tell me, Judith, what sort of suitcase she was
carrying.'

Hesitation; she touched her lower lip with her tongue.

'Come along, now. I'm not asking you to remember the

Treaty of Utrecht.'

'It was a battered old green fibre thing, with one clasp twisted open. She'd had to break into it once, when she lost the key.'

'Inspector Wright?'

'Brand new,' Shiner said. 'Plastic—looking like leather.'

'Of course. Of course. If Susan's parents thought that she was going to be asked to spend the night as a guest in a training college, they wouldn't let her go with the thing that got bust up on the last college outing. Sorry, Judith. You weren't there. Of all the incidents quoted in that ludicrous editorial, yours was the only one that only had one witness. And you were the only one telling a forthright lie.'

Justin made a desperate effort.

'It was just a journalistic trick, Mr Kenworthy. We were just trying to needle you people, to get you on the ball.'

'And how excellently it worked, didn't it? Just look at what sort of thing happens when we *are* on the ball. Oh, please don't apologize. I'll let you into a little secret about police methods. We're always delighted when someone asks to withdraw a previous statement. Sometimes it happens so often that people get confused, and have to start telling the truth to clear the air.'

He moved towards the door.

'I'll love you and leave you, then. Inspector Wright has all sorts of boring things to do—like cautioning you, and telling your parents that you're helping him, and not likely to be home tonight—'

Kenworthy was tired. Probably for the remainder of his days his warhorse nostrils would quiver whenever there was a human pattern to be recomposed from a flimsy web of observable facts. But there were some aspects of police work that he was grateful never to have to face again.

Like interrogation: the long night, the bleary-eyed, aching-backed, bristle-chinned dawn. Keeping two suspects apart; the forced patience of taking fresh statements from scratch when old ones needed amendment; the playing off of one against the other; the downright lies — telling one that the other had coughed; the ruinous bewilderment of the alternative nice-guy-and-bastard routine; the sudden confrontation of the two when something crucial had been laid bare.

Kenworthy did not doubt that Shiner would sort those two out. He knew his job; Kenworthy had trained him. And, after all, they were only kids; the very nature of their conceited cleverness was a weapon to use against them, like using a wrestler's own weight to throw him.

Quite illicitly, Shiner sent him a photocopy of the actual statements through the post.

And Kenworthy had managed to get some of his facts right. The prelude had been as he had guessed it: Susan telling Judith about her London trip, and the pair of them fixing to go to the theatre together, Susan making the hotel booking.

But then Justin had come into the action, had poured scorn on *Jesus Christ Superstar* — which he himself had already seen, anyway. Susan had met the pair of them in Charing Cross Road, not all that long after she had eaten a high tea with Everard. The three of them had gone into a pub, Susan sticking to bitter lemon in spite of her atypical mood of rebellion. That was when Justin slipped the drug into her glass: if they were going to be stuck with the Shires filly at a party, they would at least get her into an interesting state.

Susan started to get worried about the time when they still made no move, ten minutes before curtain-up, to go over to the theatre. And this was where her fundamental weakness persisted. Some girls would have said, 'I don't know about you two, but I'm going.' Susan sat unhappily waiting for them to drink up. When they came out of the pub, the show had already started; she was fated never to see it.

They went to a tatty Victorian villa-flat somewhere between Regent's Park and Camden Town. The party was based on two boys whom Susan knew, both old collegians who had left at the end of the previous summer term. One of them was a trainee technician in a hospital path. lab, the other was at the LSE. There were others present, including Freddy, an ambulance driver of ingenious whimsicality. These others were now accounting for themselves as accessories and, more importantly for Shiner, were contributing their own share of evidence.

It took some three quarters of an hour for the drug to begin to take effect on Susan, and it was then quickly apparent that she was in for a hell of a trip. Clearly her entire personality was scrambled; and so was her view of the world. She became a problem, of which the solution seemed at first to play along with her. But then she went berserk with a breadknife.

It was a sort of ballet that she attempted. Perhaps she was remembering Sergeant Troy's swordplay in *Far from the Madding Crowd*. She lunged, feinted with the thing, traced wild arabesques, attacked various creatures in the room of whose existence only she was aware. When those creatures took the form of reptiles climbing over others' shoulders, the joke began to look very sick indeed. Freddy was cut across the knuckles in trying to disarm her and shouted angrily to Justin, who was tending to stand aside from the scrimmage.

'Do something, for God's sake, Fairbrother. She's your responsibility.'

Justin tried to get the weapon off her and it grazed his sweater under the armpit. He had to go for her savagely then, had to hurt her, and she struggled back with a physical strength that he had not suspected. In the next phase of the bout, fighting now for his own life, he thrust the back of her neck against the corner of a mock Adam mantelpiece. She dropped the knife and fell herself, with a lifelessness that was at first greeted with universal relief. They carried her over to a sofa, but there was something more than merely drugged in the uncoordinated sagging of her limbs. Freddy, called from the kitchen, where he was sluicing his hand, felt her pulse and signalled that matters were as grave as they could possibly be. Her chin lolled forward and sideways over her left breast. One of her cervical vertebrae was out of alignment, as irrevocably as when done to men in vintage execution sheds.

There was temporary panic, a division of opinions. Then came clear decision and team action, prompted by a single voice speaking what was at once acclaimed to be sound sense: Freddy, the ambulance man. They had all been drinking, but none of them was out of control. Some of them were sobered by what had happened; others seemed oddly stimulated, as if it were some dream game they were playing. Question: how does one transport a body at night through the streets of an active city without any appearance of abnormality? Answer: in an ambulance. Freddy, whose bedsitter was on the same landing, had a spare suit of uniform to lend to Justin. His vehicle, in the hospital ambulance park, was locked, its key in a security office. But Freddy, a lively man, with his eye always on future contingencies, had had himself a private one cut months ago, never knowing what might arise. He and Justin did all the real work; Judith travelled with them as lookout. The others stayed in the flat, fortifying themselves with more drink, but with a tendency now to talk in whispers.

Freddy chose the building site, having recently been out there to an accident case. He drove with his blue light flashing and his siren clearing a way for them. They had adventures. It was easy and unquestioned to carry a body out of a flat on a stretcher; easy even to bring the mock-loaded stretcher back from the site. But taking Susan out to the rubble, across a pavement and along fifty yards of alleyway between buildings, could not possibly be made to look natural. Judith was posted, and they had to cover up two false starts in the face of casual pedestrians. They buried the body shallowly, and in the course of the hurried committal it was involved in indignities that were to give the first impression of multiple injuries.

By the time they arrived back in the flat, the gathering bore no more resemblance to a party. And all the liquor was gone.

Everard took sick leave. He wanted to go back to the college, at least for a short time. Dr Shepherd proposed to put no difficulties in his way, and was sure he could answer for the governors. With Justin and Judith out of the way, Everard did not doubt that he could return to a normal job of work. That would surely be better, he reasoned, than adding to his traumatic burden the self-accusation of running away. But he would stay only a few months, then he would retire early. He thought perhaps he might try his hand at writing, beginning with a novella.

The Everards invited the Kenworthys to dinner: a meal table that could have been photographed for a woman's magazine — though afterwards two men smoking pipes wrought havoc with the ashtrays. Elspeth reciprocated, and the Everards were persuaded to stay the night; it proved a long evening, and the morning bathroom routines were dislocated in a manner that the Kenworthys never seemed to notice with their usual visitors.

It was in the early days of next June that the Kenworthys had a picture postcard from Italy: a village in the province of Venezia, a goat track hairpinning down the flank of an Alp, past a rough-hewn church and a huddle of rock-perched smallholdings.

Both Everards had signed it. Perhaps Blanche had been tempted to stay down on the Austrian side to read a historical romance; but she was a woman whose sense of duty did not desert her at critical moments.